CUE ROMANCE

Michaela Trueman

CONTENTS

*For my snooker practice partner, who
taught me how to play for fun.*

PROLOGUE

About two years before...

Every time Cecilia visited her favourite cafe, on Moulsham Street, she was there. "She" was the beautiful ginger-haired girl who always had her head stuck in a book. Cecilia also always had her head stuck in a book when she was in the cafe, but her books were proof copies of crime and adventure novels, whereas the ginger girl seemed to read nothing but library copies of medical textbooks.

The cafe was the thing Cecilia would miss the most when she moved to Colchester in two weeks time. The thing she would miss most about the cafe was not the coffee, for it was cheap and you could tell; she would miss the ginger girl, who she often smiled at, but had never had the pleasure of speaking to.

The phrases "What's the worst that can happen?" and "You don't want to end up on your deathbed regretting all the things you didn't do", floated around in Cecilia's head when she looked at the girl, as did thoughts that made her blush.

Unable to ignore these thoughts, Cecilia removed herself from the queue she had been standing in, waiting to order, and made her way to the ginger girl's table for two, which was crammed into the cafe's little front window.

The ginger girl looked up from her book. 'Can I help you?' she asked.

Cecilia had never heard the girl speak before, so her rich and slow accent, from somewhere in the West Country, came as a surprise. A pleasant surprise. It just made the girl even more attractive. She definitely *could* help Cecilia.

'I want to buy you a drink, so I came over to ask what coffee you like?' Cecilia said.

'That's very kind, but why would you want to do that? You don't know me,' the girl replied. Then she chuckled to herself and added: 'I don't *think* you know me. I'm not great with faces. Sorry if I've forgotten you.'

'It's okay, you don't know me. We've never spoken before, but I've noticed you every time I've been here. You're the most beautiful woman I've ever seen. Your hair is most unruly, but in a stylish way, and your eyes are captivating. Even the way you sit, cross-legged with your head down in a book, is attractive to me. You're in your own little world, and I'd love to have a glimpse into it,' Cecilia told the girl.

Every compliment Cecilia paid the girl made her blush. 'Are you interested in me romantically?' the girl asked.

The question made Cecilia's heart flutter. 'Most definitely. As I say, you're beautiful,' she replied, wearing her biggest smile.

The girl blushed harder and sighed. 'Erm, well, I'm really sorry, but I... I just don't feel the same,' she told Cecilia.

The heart that Cecilia had felt fluttering in her chest seemed to sink into her strappy black heels. 'I understand. Sorry for bothering you,' she murmured, turning away from the girl.

'You *didn't* bother me, and *I'm* the one who should be sorry. I'm sure you're a lovely woman,' the girl called after Cecilia.

-

It took Cecilia a few minutes to get to the front of the queue. That gave her time to prepare the exact change for her order. 'It is always nice to see you,' said the man behind the counter when she got to him.

'You too, Tom. Can I get two cream teas today?' Cecilia replied.

Tom raised an eyebrow. 'Ooh, got company have you, or are you just greedy?' he asked with a smile.

'One of them is for the girl who's tucked herself away in the corner. I'm buying it to say sorry for interrupting her obviously important studies to chat her up. The other is a commiseration to myself because she turned me down,' Cecilia told Tom.

'In that case, I hope this is the best cream tea you've ever had,' Tom replied.

Once Cecilia had paid for her cream teas, she stood to one side and read an email from a client. A deadline had moved, but it was of no concern to her. She replied to the email to tell the client she had already finished proofreading the book that the deadline concerned.

It didn't take Tom long to put a metal pot of tea, a pot of strawberry jam, a pot of clotted cream, a pot of butter, two mugs, two knives, and two scones on a tray.

With her tray of cream teas, Cecilia made her way across the cafe to where the ginger girl was sitting. The tray was heavy, so she was relieved when she was able to set it down on the girl's table.

'When I said I don't have romantic feelings, I meant it. Cream tea won't change that, no matter how delicious it looks and smells,' the girl said.

Cecilia smiled at the girl. 'I know. I still think you're beautiful, but I'm not going to pursue you. I know when no means no. I just thought that as I'd have got you a coffee if you'd have said you did feel the same way as me, then I should still get you something. After all, it's not your fault you're not attracted to me. Judging by your accent, you're from the West Country, so I thought, if you're a stereotypical Cornish or Devonian girl, then you'd like this,' she replied.

This made the girl smile. 'Oh, that's lovely! Thank you! I'm *not* a stereotypical Cornish girl *at all*, but I do love cream tea! Take a seat and we'll dig in!' she cried. Evidently, she did love cream tea, a lot.

'Are you sure you don't mind me sitting with you? I was going to take mine to my own table so I didn't bother you any more. Surely I've taken enough of your time already?' Cecilia said.

'Trust me, you're not bothering me. Unless you have an ulterior motive or something, I'd love the company. I'm desperately lonely. Besides, this has been made up to share. There's only one teapot and one set of jam and cream,' the girl replied.

As it happened, Cecilia was lonely too. 'You know what, I'd like the company too,' she declared, sitting down opposite the girl.

With a huge grin on her face, the ginger girl cut her scone open and then spread a generous helping of cream on it. Then, with some difficulty, she spread jam on that.

'Before I stuff my face, I should probably introduce myself. My name is Cecilia,' Cecilia said.

For a few seconds, the ginger girl left her scone alone to extend her hand and say: 'Nice to meet you, Cecilia. I'm Tamsyn.'

*

CHAPTER ONE

If Jude aimed his shot correctly, he was sure to defeat Morton. If it missed, Jude's hopes of getting one up on his long-time foe would be dashed.

To ensure it was successful, Jude focused his mind and looked down the line of his shot. It looked perfect, so he drew a deep breath and took the shot. The white ball rolled across the table and smashed into the black ball, which rattled in the jaws.

'Ha! You lose yet again!' Morton crowed.

Jude didn't hear his friend jeer at him. He was still down on his shot, looking at the intriguing blonde who was the reason he'd missed it.

The game of snooker, which Jude and Morton were playing, requires its players to bend over vast cloth-covered tables and stare intently at the ball they intend to hit with the cue ball, which they hit with their cue, a long wooden stick. That was how Jude had ended up in an impromptu staring contest with the woman playing on the next table. He stood stock-still, gazing into the woman's blue eyes, while she gazed right back at him, standing in a similar position to him.

Because only two of the six tables were in use, and they were being used by three quiet people, the snooker room at the Colneside was silent. The temporary silence in the room was broken by the soft donk of a cue striking the cue ball, followed by the click of the cue ball making contact with the object ball, and the growl of frustration from the woman who had set that chain of events in motion. She immediately stood up, thus breaking eye contact with Jude, who realised the woman had been staring at the ball she'd been aiming to pot, not him. There had never been a staring contest, but if there had been one, he'd have won it.

'Go on then. Humiliate me yet again,' Jude said to Morton, walking away from the table to let him take his shot.

A great deal of noise came from the table next to the one Morton was playing on because the woman using it was setting all the balls up again, but that didn't put him off his shot. He sent the black ball spinning nine feet across the baize and into the corner pocket with perfect accuracy.

'Did you mean like that?' Morton asked.

'Yup. Pretty much that,' Jude confirmed.

Morton glanced at his watch. 'We've got plenty of time left. Shall we set up again?' he suggested.

'That's cool with me. I'll do the baulk colours. As you're the one who potted most of them, you can do the reds and the colours down your end,' Jude agreed.

The pair strolled to their respective ends of the table to do just that. As he walked, it occurred to Morton that something was wrong with what Jude had said, and he couldn't help but mention it. 'Actually, you potted more of the balls. You took lower value colours with your reds, so although your score was lower than mine, you scored it with more balls,' he pointed out.

In response, Jude stuck his tongue out and said: 'Dweeb.'

Instead of continuing to insult Morton, Jude put all his concentration into putting the yellow, brown, and green balls on the white spots marked for them on the snooker table.

At the opposite end of the table, Morton was methodically putting the fifteen red balls into the wooden triangle provided for them.

On the table next to Jude and Morton, the woman playing on it had finished setting it up. She placed the cue ball precisely where she wanted it, next to the brown ball, and bent double over the snooker table. Full of hope, but not much confidence, the woman struck the cue ball with the battered cue she'd picked up from the rack on the wall by her table. She stayed bent over the table to watch the cue ball merrily roll straight past the triangle of reds it was supposed to glance off, bounce off of a couple of the cushions at the edge of the table, and come straight back to her. 'Seriously!' she yelled.

The sheer frustration in the one word the woman spoke, and the volume she spoke it in, attracted the attention of Jude and Morton. They glanced in her direction and saw she had her head in her hands. 'I can't do this. I just can't do this,' they heard her mutter to herself.

'Erm, don't wanna intrude or nothing, but are you alright?' Jude couldn't help asking the woman.

'Oh, I'm sorry for bothering you. I'm fine, just most frustrated that I can't do this,' the woman replied.

Jude and Morton looked at each other. Morton raised an eyebrow as if he was asking a question, but Jude didn't know what the question was. When Jude didn't answer the question, whatever it was, Morton tutted and turned his attention to the woman. 'Would you like me to give you a few pointers? I've been doing this a long time and I've learnt a lot over that time. I can't impart my wealth of knowledge to Jude here, because he just won't listen, but you'd probably be a more willing pupil,' Morton offered.

Only then did Jude realise that Morton's unspoken question to him had been: "Shall we help her?".

While the woman was considering Morton's offer, a man and woman entered the snooker room, kissing each other noisily as they walked. They made their way to the end table, which thankfully was as far away from Jude and Morton as possible.

'That would be most helpful. Thank you,' the woman who Morton had spoken to replied.

A smile appeared on Morton's face. 'Fantabulous! I'm Morton, by the way, and my friend here is called Jude,' Morton said.

'My name is Cecilia,' said the woman, who was called Cecilia.

-

As it happened, Morton had more than "a few" pointers. He critiqued and tweaked every part of Cecilia's game, from her stance, to where she placed her left hand on the table. He also talked her through what to consider when deciding what shot to play.

Much to Morton's delight, Cecilia listened to his every word and did exactly as she was told. After an hour's intensive tuition, Cecilia felt much more confident and capable in the game of snooker.

While Morton coached Cecilia, Jude stood nonchalantly in the background and watched him do it. It was his intention to say something clever and funny to impress the alluring Cecilia, but he didn't get the chance as she was completely and utterly focused on what Morton was teaching her. That was probably for the best because despite having an hour to think about it, Jude didn't come up with anything clever or funny to say.

Jude, Morton, and Cecilia only became aware of the time when the woman of the once-noisily kissing couple mentioned how late it was and suggested that, as they both had uni tomorrow, they really should go to bed. The man of the couple replied: 'You mean together, right?' That inspired the woman to kiss him noisily again.

'I definitely should head home. I've got piles of work to get through tomorrow,' Cecilia said.

Jude nodded thoughtfully. 'Yeah, and I've got to see a client in the morning,' he added.

As if agreeing, Morton yawned. 'Then we should all pay up and return to our respective homes,' he declared.

'Thank you, guys. I'm most grateful for the tips you gave me, Morton, and you, poor Jude, must have been bored standing around by yourself because I'd taken your friend away from you,' Cecilia said

'I usually am bored when I'm out with Morton,' Jude commented.

Cecilia chuckled to herself. 'Goodnight, guys,' she said, walking out of the snooker room.

-

A minute later, after downing their vodka and colas, Jude and Morton followed in Cecilia's footsteps.

'Same again next week, my friend?' Morton asked Jude while they stood at the snooker club bar, waiting to pay.

'Yup, just like every week,' Jude agreed.

*

CHAPTER TWO

'Hey, Cecilia!' Jude called to Cecilia when she walked into the snooker room at the Colneside half an hour after he and Morton had.

Behind Cecilia, a young woman with short ginger hair and long legs who looked a couple of years younger than her companion walked in. 'Ah, do you know these men?' the ginger girl asked in a thick West Country accent.

'Vaguely. Morton, on the left, helped me improve my game, and Jude, with the brown curly hair and grey eyes, waited patiently while he did so,' Cecilia told her companion.

The ginger girl nodded. 'Nice to meet you, Jude and Morton. I'm Tamsyn,' she said.

'One day to be Tamsyn Menadue BA (Hons),' Cecilia added.

Tamsyn blushed. 'Well, I don't know about that,' she replied.

With the intention of making Cecilia laugh, Jude bowed low. 'A pleasure to make your acquaintance, Miss Menadue, one day to be BA (Hons),' he said.

A quiet titter came from Cecilia, but Tamsyn just silently folded her arms. 'I assume that was meant to be funny,' she said.

'Yup, it was. Didn't quite work out how I hoped,' Jude replied.

'Well I was amused,' Cecilia told Jude.

'Good. It was my aim to amuse you. Beautiful women like you deserve to be amused,' Jude revealed.

'Beautiful?' Cecilia questioned.

A slight smile broke out on Jude's face. 'Yeah. You're beautiful, among other things I imagine. I'm single, among other things,' he replied.

While wondering how to answer that, Cecilia felt Tamsyn tugging at her arm. She let herself be dragged to the snooker table next to Jude and Morton's, which was already lit for their use.

'Right then. Shall we get back to business? It was your shot, I believe,' Morton said to Jude, forcing him to turn his attention back to the game.

Giving Cecilia one last wistful look, Jude walked around his snooker table and got down on his shot.

—

Like last week, Jude was distracted by the table next to him, so couldn't concentrate on his own game. He noticed that Cecilia was playing a little better than the week before, and she was a lot calmer.

At one point, after Tamsyn missed a shot for the third time, she burst out laughing, and Cecilia tittered with her.

'Thank you for coming with me to practice,' Cecilia said to Tamsyn when their laughter had subsided.

'We both know you asked me here for my benefit, for which I'm extremely grateful. The last thing I felt like doing after that phone call was studying, but that's exactly what I'd have done if you hadn't called,' Tamsyn replied.

'Then it suits both of us,' Cecilia declared.

After five attempts, Tamsyn played her shot correctly and so it was Cecilia's turn to play. All Tamsyn had been able to do was hit a red ball; she hadn't been able to put the cue ball somewhere where Cecilia wouldn't be able to pot. She had left a straight pot to the middle pocket. In the game of snooker, pots didn't get much easier than that, so Cecilia was furious with herself when she hit the red just off centre, sending it to one side of the pocket.

'I'm awful! Conner is sure to laugh at me!' Cecilia cried.

'You're not *awful*. Even if you *were*, it's just a game,' Tamsyn told Cecilia.

'A game Conner is sure to beat me at,' Cecilia replied.

Tamsyn shrugged. '*If* he beats you, and *if* he laughs at you, just remember that it says so much more about him then it does about you,' she said.

A wave of guilt suddenly overcame Cecilia. 'I'm sorry for moaning about family. They're nothing compared to yours,' she replied.

'True, but mine are three hundred miles away. Of course, that doesn't stop my mother calling me up out of the blue to ask: "When are you going to find yourself a nice guy, or even a girl. We'd understand you know, if it's a girl. We get that is part of the modern world that we live in now. Perhaps that's why you still haven't found someone. You're one of those lesbian people",' Tamsyn pointed out, hamming up her accent when she quoted her mother.

Even that short snippet of Tamsyn's phone call with her mother angered Cecilia. 'They're lucky that they live three hundred miles away, for it makes it too difficult for me to drive to their house and strangle them,' she growled.

Tamsyn cackled at the idea of Cecilia strangling her parents. 'Well, that would give me resus practice I suppose,' she said.

Even though Jude knew eavesdropping was rude, he couldn't help listening to every word of Cecilia and Tamsyn's conversation. He was in fact so tuned in to them that he didn't hear Morton asking him a question. He did hear him when he hissed in his ear: 'Did you not notice that she completely ignored it when you said you were single? Sorry, but she's not interested, my friend.'

'Like you know anything about relationships. Remind me, how long have you been single? Twenty-one years, ain't it?' Jude retorted.

Colour drained from Morton's face. 'Um, well... that is true, but it's... well it's just...,' he stammered.

'An incredibly mean thing to say?' Jude suggested.

Morton nodded, but still couldn't find the words.

Some people might hug at this moment, but Jude wasn't much of a hugger. Instead of hugging the now-miserable Morton, he half-heartedly slapped him on the back. 'I don't mean to upset you. I were just joshing with you, you know? I don't think sometimes before I open my gob,' Jude told his friend.

A slight smile appeared on Morton's face. 'That... that is very... really true,' he agreed.

'What's best for you now? Do you want to carry on or is it better to call the whole thing off?' Jude asked.

'Go home. This isn't going to... to go away,' Morton replied.

That was the answer Jude had expected. He knew Morton well, and he knew when his stammer made an appearance, it ruined everything for him, even his beloved snooker. That was why Jude felt sick with guilt for inadvertently causing Morton to stammer.

'Okay then. I'll collect the balls, take them back to the man and pay up, so you can go if you like. I'll see you next week, if you wanna see me next week, that is,' Jude said.

'Yes, just like every week,' Morton replied.

*

CHAPTER THREE

Sometimes Tamsyn loved living in a shared house. One of those times was when she got to cook with Scott, one of her house-mates.

'The trick to a good macaroni cheese sauce is to whisk, whisk, whisk,' Scott said, doing just that.

Somehow, Scott managed to send a glob of the slowly thickening sauce flying onto Tamsyn's jumper.

'Hey!' Tamsyn cried, grabbing a piece of kitchen towel to get the sauce off of her jumper.

'Okay, maybe don't whisk it that much,' Scott recommended with a smile.

'Oh, you think so(?) I'm so going to get you back for that at pool tonight,' Tamsyn replied.

The fury on Tamsyn's face amused Scott. He laughed at her. 'What you gonna do?' he asked through his laughter.

-

At the Waves and Receiver pub in Chelmsford two hours after eating the macaroni cheese that he hadn't thrown on Tamsyn's jumper, Scott found out exactly how she planned to get her revenge when she played a shot perfectly so that the cue ball ended up tight on the cushion.

'Ugh! You know I hate cuing off the cushion,' Scott whined when he saw the shot Tamsyn had left him with.

'Serves you right for potentially ruining my favourite jumper,' Tamsyn replied.

Just as Tamsyn had hoped, Scott failed to hit any object balls with his poorly struck cue ball.

'Foul! I get two shots,' Tamsyn announced to everyone in earshot.

'You know if I *have* ruined your jumper that I'll get you another one,' Scott said.

Tamsyn nodded. 'Yes, I do. That's why I'm laughing about it with you,' she replied.

There was a pause in the conversation while Tamsyn sent the last yellow ball on the table into the nearest pocket. She then did the same with the black ball.

Having defeated Scott, Tamsyn turned her attention back to him. 'Won't stop me winning though,' she told him.

'*Nothing* will stop you winning, Tamsyn. You are a force to be reckoned with, on the pool table for sure, but probably also at uni, on ambulances, and everywhere else in life,' Scott replied.

"A force to be reckoned with," was exactly what Tamsyn aspired to be.

*

CHAPTER FOUR

In some people's opinion, including Emma-Leigh Layton's, the shop-lined Lanes south of the High Street were the best parts of Colchester. That was why she had taken her old school friend, Cecilia Bradley, there. Together, they hoped to find the perfect outfit for Cecilia's upcoming meeting with her brother, Conner.

'As far as I understand it, snooker involves a lot of bending, so we're not looking for a little black dress here. Am I right?' Emma-Leigh asked.

Cecilia nodded emphatically. 'Definitely. You're one hundred percent right. I need trousers,' she agreed.

While Emma-Leigh tried to conjure up an image of a stylish outfit that somehow incorporated trousers, she pouted. Emma-Leigh always pouted when she concentrated. Her nickname in school had been "Little Miss Pouty Face" because of it.

For no discernible reason, Emma-Leigh stopped walking and clicked her fingers. 'That's it! A power suit!' she cried.

'Like Thatcher?' Cecilia questioned.

Emma-Leigh wasn't listening to Cecilia anymore; she wasn't even with her. She was pressed up against the window of a contemporary fashion boutique.

When Cecilia noticed Emma-Leigh's absence, she ran up to her.

'Ah, good, you've caught up. I've just seen the perfect thing,' Emma-Leigh said to Cecilia when she reached her.

Before Cecilia could ask what the perfect thing was, Emma-Leigh marched into the shop, so she had to just follow her into it.

Behind the counter of the shop was a twenty-something young lady with a flawless face of natural look make-up who was wearing an immaculate white dress. The young lady looked Cecilia and Emma-Leigh up and down and smirked. 'We have nothing for you. I think you're in the wrong place. Please leave immediately,' she said to them.

'Seriously?' Emma-Leigh asked, putting her hands on her hips.

The smirk on the shop assistant's face turned into a proper smile that seemed to alter her whole appearance for the better. 'No, not seriously. Like I would ever say that to anyone. I work on commission,' she said.

When neither Cecilia nor Emma-Leigh laughed at her film reference, the shop assistant cleared her throat and made a sweeping gesture at the rails in the shop, which were packed with a wide variety of clothes. 'We have lots of things for you, and any woman who walks in here I should think,' she told them.

'Oh, well, that is what I thought,' Emma-Leigh replied.

The shop assistant couldn't think of an answer to this. The way she'd greeted Cecilia and Emma-Leigh had created a stilted atmosphere between them.

In an attempt to heal the damage her greeting had done, the shop assistant decided to start from scratch, as if nothing had happened. 'Welcome to Toothill's. I'm Eugenie. How can I help you?' she asked.

Emma-Leigh frowned. 'I'm Emma-Leigh, and you can help us by finding my friend Cecilia here a nice outfit that she can play snooker in,' she replied.

'Nice to meet you Emily and Cecilia. I'd love to find you a nice outfit to play snooker in. What sort of thing are you into, Cecilia?' Eugenie asked.

Emma-Leigh folded her arms. 'It's not *Emily*, it's *Emma-Leigh*. I did say that,' she pointed out.

'Ah, erm, yes, sorry. I haven't really got off to a good start here, have I?' Eugenie replied.

Before Emma-Leigh could open her mouth to confirm that Eugenie had indeed not got off to a good start, Cecilia came to her rescue. 'I would describe my style as smart, but somewhat practical. Definitely conservative, but with a small c. I do *not* want to look like Thatcher or May,' she told the young shop assistant.

A smile appeared on Eugenie's face because she knew exactly what to pick out for Cecilia.

'What size are you, if you don't mind me asking?' Eugenie enquired.

'Fourteen, I think. At least I hope that's what I am. It was the last time I checked, but I have been a bit of a pig recently. I have eyes bigger than my belly,' Cecilia replied.

Armed with all the information she required, Eugenie danced around the little shop, deftly removing a pair of baby blue smart trousers, matching waistcoat, and a white silk shirt from the rails. She ended her dance with a flourish by draping the clothes over the counter for Cecilia to see.

'This should be perfect! I used to watch snooker, and I remember that the players wear shirts and waistcoats, so I know this outfit is practical. The pale colour should go with your *amazing* blonde hair and bring out your pretty eyes,' Eugenie explained.

'I don't see any shoes,' Emma-Leigh commented.

'I don't *need* shoes. I have those cream shoe boots at home. The heel on them is quite blocky, so hopefully I shouldn't fall over and embarrass myself,' Cecilia said.

It always pleased Eugenie when people started accessorising around an outfit she'd chosen for them. It showed that they could picture themselves wearing it.

'Sounds perfect. Would you like to give this lot a new home

then?' Eugenie asked.

'I haven't shown you the suit that drew me into the shop yet,' Emma-Leigh pointed out.

There was a reason why Emma-Leigh hadn't shown Cecilia the suit yet. That reason was that Cecilia didn't particularly want to see it, so she'd been pretending to have forgotten all about it. She couldn't say this without offending her friend though.

An idea came to Cecilia that meant she could leave the shop without offending Emma-Leigh or taking home the suit that she didn't want.

'I need to try this lot on anyway, simply to make sure it fits. If it doesn't look good on me, which it might not, then I'll try the power suit you spotted,' Cecilia told Emma-Leigh.

'A good decision. I assume they have a fitting room here,' Emma-Leigh agreed.

'We *do*. It is in the far corner. If you tell me your shoe size, then I'll give you some boots that are similar to the ones you de-scribed. That way you can see how it all looks,' Eugenie said.

-

'I don't think we'll be looking at my beloved power suit,' Emma-Leigh said when Cecilia emerged from the fitting room.

Eugenie thought the outfit looked so good on Cecilia that she clapped her hands and squealed. 'I *love it* when a plan comes to-gether!' she cried.

There was a full-length mirror on the wall next to the counter. Cecilia used it to look at herself, for that was the purpose of the mirror.

'I like it. I really like it. You certainly know how to do your job,' Cecilia said.

Being complimented always made Eugenie smile. Being complimented on her work made her *beam*.

'Thank you. I'm so glad you like it,' Eugenie replied.

'The boots were a nice touch. They help me properly see how this is all going to look. It was very clever of you to give them to me,' Cecilia said, looking down at her boot-clad feet.

Eugenie's smile grew even wider. 'Thank you, but it's not my idea. I think it's quite common practice to give people shoes to try on with their clothes. Not just because it's helpful, but also because the shop hopes you'll buy the shoes you wore while trying stuff on,' she revealed. 'Obviously, *you* won't buy the boots, because you already have similar ones, but that's *usually* the idea,' Eugenie added, feeling the need to further explain herself.

Because they were being discussed, and she was being ignored, Emma-Leigh took a closer look at the boots. She noticed several differences between them and the cream heeled shoe boots that Cecilia already had. This gave her a thought.

'Well, now that you know you like this outfit, why don't you take it off again so you can get it home? You can take the boots off in here of course. It won't hurt to walk the few feet to the fitting room barefoot,' Emma-Leigh said.

Even though she would soon own the clothes, so could wear them as often as she wished, Cecilia was reluctant to take them off. She felt so comfortable in them. She gazed at herself in the mirror one last time before she answered Emma-Leigh.

'I suppose you're right, Emma-Leigh. I'll slip these boots off to give back to you, Eugenie,' Cecilia eventually said, doing just that.

As soon as Cecilia was in the fitting room, Emma-Leigh leaned conspiratorially across the counter. 'I want to buy these for her,' she whispered to Eugenie.

'Doesn't she already have boots just like them?' Eugenie questioned.

'These are much prettier than hers. The toes on hers are more rounded, and hers are not leather. They can be her birthday present ,' Emma-Leigh replied.

-

By the time Cecilia returned to the counter, wearing the clothes she'd entered the shop in, the boots were safely tucked away in a paper shopping bag held by Emma-Leigh.

'I might have known you'd get something. You can't walk into a shop and not buy something, can you?' Cecilia said when she saw Emma-Leigh's bag.

'You know me too well,' Emma-Leigh replied.

'What did you get?' Cecilia asked.

Emma-Leigh and Eugenie shared a smile.

'I'll tell you outside,' Emma-Leigh said.

-

'There are some things about this town that I love. To be specific, I love the little independent boutiques, the friendly staff that work in them, and the clothes they sell,' Cecilia commented to Emma-Leigh as they walked down one of Colchester's many narrow streets.

Ahead of Cecilia and Emma-Leigh, curled up on the pavement in a doorway, was a man in a sleeping bag.

'There are some things I don't love about this town,' Emma-Leigh replied, looking in the direction of the doorway.

Cecilia frowned. 'It's so sad. I wish someone would do something to help,' she said.

Like most people, Cecilia and Emma-Leigh looked the other way when they passed the man in the doorway. He was asleep, so unaware of this.

'Do you feel better about tomorrow now you have such a good outfit?' Emma-Leigh asked Cecilia once they were past the sleeping man.

Cecilia nodded and said: 'Yes, definitely. It's funny how clothes can give you confidence.'

*

CHAPTER FIVE

There were many heads in the snooker room at the Colneside, and all of them turned when Cecilia entered. Most of the time, attracting that much attention unsettled Cecilia. She'd usually wonder if she'd smudged her make-up, committed a fashion faux-pas or even worse, had a wardrobe malfunction.

Today, the attention made Cecilia smile for she knew it was thanks to her outfit, and how much it suited her. That was the joy of having someone else pick out clothes for her. She had absolute confidence that Eugenie from Toothill's had chosen the right outfit for her. She didn't even question if the attention it was attracting was positive; she knew it was. If Cecilia had chosen the outfit herself, she wouldn't feel so comfortable.

Unlike most of the people in the room, Jude's attention wasn't gripped by the nice clothes, but by the person wearing them. His only thought about the clothes was: '*Why has she gone to such an effort?*'. It was a question Jude would have liked to know the answer to, but he didn't ask it. To him, it seemed too personal an enquiry.

'My, you know how to dress, if you don't mind me saying so. May I ask if you've gone to all this effort for someone in particular?' Morton asked Cecilia.

'I'm wearing these clothes for me, not who I'm meeting. It's kind of you to say I know how to dress, but I don't. Eugenie from one of the boutiques in the Lanes picked this lot out for me,' Cecilia replied.

'You wear them well,' Jude commented. He hadn't intended to comment on Cecilia's attire, but as always with Jude, his words left his mouth without any prior consideration.

There was nothing Cecilia wanted to say to that, so she didn't answer Jude. She didn't want to *thank* him. Thanking Jude would suggest she was grateful for his comment, and she *wasn't*. She didn't need him to tell her she wore the clothes well. The comment didn't irritate her though because she saw nothing wrong with it. It was just unnecessary.

When Cecilia started setting up her table, everyone else in the room got back to doing whatever they were doing before she'd walked in, which for everyone except the young couple at one end, was playing snooker. The young couple at the end had been kissing , and as everyone could hear, they picked up where they left off.

-

One of the best and worst things about snooker is that only one person can play at a time because you play on the same table. If you're doing well, your opponent has to sit and watch you. *Conversely*, if your *opponent* is doing well, *you* have to sit and watch *them*.

It was perfectly normal for Jude to spend the majority of his time at the Colneside leaning on the wall, watching Morton play snooker. This didn't bother him. He had a drink which was mildly alcoholic, he exchanged the occasional witty remark with Morton (Jude was always the one to make the witty remark, in his opinion), and he did play some shots every couple of minutes or so. Morton was good, but not flawless. Even professional snooker players aren't flawless. More recently, watching Cecilia had been another form of entertainment for Jude.

Today, Jude was spending more than a few minutes at a time off the table. Morton was in top form.

'I'm sorry, my friend. Do you want me to play an unnecessary safety every now and again so you can play a little bit?' Morton asked after potting twenty-four balls in a row to make a break of eighty-four.

'Nah, mate, you're on one tonight. Don't break your flow. I'm fine here. It's just cool to see you enjoying yourself,' Jude replied.

'As long as you're sure. I must admit, I'm having a whale of a time, as they say,' Morton said.

With Jude's help, Morton set the balls up for a new frame so he could keep playing.

On the table next to them, Cecilia was also setting her table up having given up on her quest to clear it. She had perfect timing, for the man she was setting it up to play with walked in just as she was placing the pink, which was the last ball she had to place before the table was ready to play on.

'Hey, little sister! Did I, and everyone else here come to think of it, miss a memo to wear formal attire?' Conner said in greeting to Cecilia.

Cecilia's face turned bright red. 'Erm, no, I just liked this,' she mumbled.

'Pardon? Seems I missed a whispering memo as well. How silly I am,' Conner said.

If at that moment the floor had opened up underneath Cecilia and swallowed her up, she'd have thanked her lucky stars. Unfortunately for her, it didn't. She was stuck in the now-stuffy-seeming snooker room with her brother, who was waiting for an answer. An answer she didn't have.

In a flash of inspiration, Cecilia came up with the perfect reply. 'I'm going on a date once we're done. I can't believe you thought this was for you,' she told Conner with a fake smile.

'Oh, I see. I didn't know you had someone. The last boyfriend I knew you to have was Nicolas, and I thought he was long gone,'

Conner replied.

'I met this man a few weeks ago, in this very room in fact,' Cecilia revealed with a genuine smile. She enjoyed seeing the irritation on Conner's face when she completely ignored the mention of her ex-boyfriend.

It took Conner quite a few seconds to respond. He usually found Cecilia to be quite predictable, but news of a new boyfriend and the lack of reaction to him mentioning her old boyfriend threw him.

'Well, this room is for playing snooker, not finding men, so shall we do that?' Conner eventually suggested.

'For now, yes, until I have to leave for my date. You can break-off,' Cecilia said.

-

As Morton was still dominating the table Jude was on, he amused himself by watching the table next to it. Despite Cecilia's best efforts, Conner got ahead on the scoreboard and there was nothing she could do to stop him steadily increasing that lead.

In an attempt to claw back control of the table, Cecilia played a shot to leave the cue ball behind the brown, which would make it very difficult for Conner to hit the red balls he needed to hit on his next shot. What Cecilia hadn't realised was that the red ball she hit to get the right angle would bounce off the cushion to hit the cue ball again, in what is known as a double kiss, thus leaving the cue ball in a completely different and very easy to play from spot.

Laughter erupted from Conner. 'That's kind of you, Cecilia, but you really don't need to make this any easier for me,' he told her.

'I didn't mean to. I made a mistake,' Cecilia replied.

'You don't say,' Conner said, getting into position to pot the straight red Cecilia had left him.

-

After potting that straight red, Conner made a break to win him the frame with a sizeable seventy point advantage.

'Remind me again why you bothered turning up, little sister?' Conner asked after potting the final black with little difficulty.

'Because you invited me here! The point of this was some brother-sister bonding time, not for you to crow over me yet again!' Cecilia snapped.

Conner took a few steps back from his sister. 'Whoa, Cecilia! Calm down! I was only teasing you. Talk about overreacting,' he said.

As always when someone challenged her, in her mind Cecilia went over the words that she and the person challenging her, Conner in this case, had exchanged. It was something she couldn't help doing. Emma-Leigh had once pointed out this habit could be a good thing, as if you have a good enough memory to recall conversations verbatim, you can throw people's own words back at them. On review, Cecilia found there were no words she could throw back at Conner. Yes, some of the things he'd said were snidey, but if she mentioned them to him then he'd just say: "I was only teasing you. Can't you take a joke?". Cecilia knew this because it had happened before.

'Forgive me. It seems one doesn't grow out of being shamefully competitive,' Cecilia said.

'Yeah, it's an inbuilt thing, isn't it? I can understand why you still struggle with losing,' Conner replied, seemingly sympathetically.

Just as Cecilia had predicted, Conner had completely misinterpreted what she'd said. She'd meant that he hadn't grown out of being shamefully competitive, hence why she'd asked for his forgiveness, because it was a rude thing to say.

'I need to pay a visit to the little boys room. You know how to set all this up again, don't you?' Conner said to Cecilia, gesturing at the now-empty snooker table. He didn't wait for an answer before walking out.

Cecilia *did* know how to set the table up for she'd looked it up, along with the rules of the game, the day Conner had suggested they play snooker together.

Before Cecilia could move a single ball, a voice beside her said: 'And breathe.'

The voice came from Jude, who, as it wasn't his turn on the table, had walked over to chat to Cecilia while her brother wasn't around.

'I am trying to stay calm. He just riles me somehow,' Cecilia replied.

'I can see why. He's not exactly polite, is he?' Jude commented.

The idea of Conner being polite made Cecilia snort. 'That is the *last* thing he is. Successful, popular, but not polite,' she said.

There was something Jude had wanted to ask Cecilia for a while, but this was the first chance he'd got. If the answer wasn't what he hoped, then he'd make things very awkward between them, but he was pretty confident that he was correct in his suspicions.

'When you mentioned going on a date with a man you met here, were you thinking of me?' Jude asked.

'Oh, yes! I'd forgotten about that! I did mean you! I meant to ask you subtly to play along, but I never got the chance!' Cecilia cried.

The door to the snooker room opened and heavy footsteps came through.

'Never got the chance to what?' Conner asked as he caught the last words Cecilia said.

Before Cecilia answered her brother she mouthed, 'Play along,' at

Jude.

In dramatic fashion, Cecilia span round to face Conner. 'I never got a chance to arrange an exact time for my date with Jude here. It's okay though because that time is now,' she replied.

*

CHAPTER SIX

Thierry's Steakhouse and Grill at The Colneside had a very unromantic atmosphere thanks to its proximity to bowling alleys full of noisy students, but as it was located underneath the snooker club they'd been playing in, that's where Jude and Cecilia went for their date.

'I can't believe I actually get to have a date with you. You know you could have said we was going on a date and then just gone home, leaving me alone,' Jude said when Cecilia lead him to a table.

'I am aware of that fact, but I'm tired of being single and you hinted that you're interested in me last week. You're not my usual "type", but I thought I may as well give you a chance. Your company can't bother me any more than that of my twin brother,' Cecilia replied, using her fingers for quotation marks.

Jude raised an eyebrow. 'You're twins? I'd never have thought so,' he said.

'Thank you, I take that as a complement. I like to think that all Conner and I have in common is a birthday,' Cecilia replied.

'That were the impression I got from where I were standing,' Jude told Cecilia.

Something made Cecilia frown, but Jude didn't notice. Even if he had have noticed, he wouldn't have known that Cecilia was frowning because she felt guilty. She didn't know why she felt guilty. Logic, and recollections of things Tamsyn and Emma-Leigh had said, told her she'd tried her best to build a good relationship with Conner. There was no good reason for her to feel guilty, but she still did.

There were laminated menus in the middle of the table, and Cecilia slid one out of its plastic stand to disguise her discomfort. She scanned the list of cuts of meat for one that was affordable and appealing. The description of the sticky BBQ chicken wings made her mouth water.

'Anything tickle your fancy? I'm paying, of course, so I'm hoping you have a thing for side salad,' Jude said. When Cecilia whipped down her menu to look at him in surprise, he laughed. 'I'm joshing with you, of course, about the side salad thing I mean. Have whatever you want,' Jude revealed.

After one last look at the menu, Cecilia made up her mind what she was going to order. 'Thank you for that. I'll have the buttermilk chicken, if that's okay,' she said.

'That's fine, if that's what you actually want. I really were joking about the salad thing. I ain't made of money, but it's not every day I get to treat a beautiful lady like yourself. I don't want you to choose one of the cheapest dishes on the menu cos you feel bad about the cost. I'm having fillet,' Jude replied.

'That's not why I'm choosing it, and I *do* mean that,' Cecilia told Jude, and that was true. She chose buttermilk chicken because she could eat it tidily, unlike the sticky BBQ chicken wings she craved so much.

Believing that Cecilia genuinely wanted buttermilk chicken, Jude went off to the bar to order it, along with fillet steak, vodka and cola, and a glass of prosecco.

-

'Got a text from Morton while I were at the bar. Apparently, he's using your twin brother as a mop,' Jude told Cecilia when he returned to their table.

'A mop, did you say? I don't understand,' Cecilia replied.

Jude chuckled. 'Yup, cos he's wiping the floor with him, get it?' he explained.

There was no response from Cecilia, so Jude assumed she didn't get it, and he was quite right. Cecilia now understood Jude's wordplay, but she didn't find it amusing.

'What I should have said were: "Morton is thoroughly beating Conner at snooker". I have a tendency to make jokes that don't come off. You might have noticed that,' Jude said.

'It might simply be that I have no sense of humour,' Cecilia suggested.

'Nah, it ain't you. No-one laughs at me. My little sister used to, but she ain't little now, and she don't find me funny no more. I suppose that as a student of philosophy at Cambridge, King's College no less, my silly humour is beneath her,' Jude replied.

Although Jude spoke in a bright and breezy tone, it was belied by his far-off expression. Cecilia could tell that this Cambridge University student sister of his mattered to him or *used* to matter to him. For that reason, she decided not to ask about her, lest she create an awkward atmosphere between her and Jude.

'Did you go to university? Are you at university now? I'm not sure how old you are,' Cecilia asked.

The suggestion that Jude could be a uni student or graduate made him laugh. 'Nah. I'm twenty-one, so by age I could be at uni, but I ain't anywhere near bright enough. I could barely pass GCSE's, so I didn't even bother with A-levels, let alone *uni*. My siblings got all the intelligence in the family,' he replied. Then, suddenly, he felt the need to add: 'Not that I care, you understand. Sure, a degree would be nice so I could get a well-paid job, but it don't really matter.'

'Indeed it does not. You should do what makes you happy,' Cecilia agreed.

It surprised Jude that Cecilia said this. To him, she looked like all the people who'd been on and on at him throughout his adolescence to "better himself". He didn't feel the need to "better himself". He felt good enough as he was. The idea of a woman who agreed with that really appealed to him.

'I assume you did go to university. You just have the sense to see you don't need to do that to be happy,' Jude said.

A frown appeared on Cecilia's face, and this time Jude noticed it. 'Don't assume. Never assume anything. It'll hurt those around you and leave you looking like an idiot. If you're unsure of something, ask. Don't just make things up,' she barked.

Jude held his hands up. 'Alright, sorry. Didn't mean to upset you,' he replied.

'No, I'm sorry. It was unnecessary to answer so harshly,' Cecilia said.

'Hey, it's forgiven. It weren't a big deal. Chillax, Cici,' Jude told Cecilia.

Suddenly, Cecilia's eyes started filling with tears. 'Don't call me that! No-one can ever call me that again!' Cecilia cried, finding it hard to speak.

To her utter mortification, Cecilia started sobbing uncontrollably.

'Oh, Cecilia! What did I do? I didn't mean to make you cry,' Jude said.

Because she was crying, Cecilia couldn't explain *why* she was crying. All she could do was get up, pull two £20 notes out of her pocket, and drop them on the table.

'Are you going? Whatever I said, I'm sorry,' Jude said.

Cecilia opened her mouth to apologise yet again, but no words came out. She shook her head and walked away, leaving Jude alone and confused with two dinners on the way.

*

CHAPTER SEVEN

Most days, Cecilia relished the time she spent home alone. She lived in a mid-terrace house, but it was peaceful for she was lucky enough to have respectful neighbours. Unfortunately, the lack of noise in her house didn't translate to peace in her mind, at least not on *that* day.

All Cecilia could think about was Jude, who she had so rudely walked out on. She'd never got the chance to exchange numbers with him, so she couldn't even call him up to apologise or explain why she'd got so upset.

From experience, Cecilia knew that if she did nothing, she would just spend all day going over and over what Jude had said, why it had upset her, and how he must have felt when she burst into tears and abandoned him. She had to do something.

The "something" Cecilia decided to do was bake. It seemed like an appropriate thing to do.

Before she had even decided what to bake or checked that she had ingredients, Cecilia removed her treasured wooden rolling pin from its drawer. Burnt into it with a pyrography pen was the message: "Happy eighteenth birthday, Cici! Lots of love, Mum".

While Cecilia was admiring her rolling pin, there was a knock at the door.

'There's no rush, Cecilia! It's me!' the person at the door called.

The thick Cornish accent of the voice told Cecilia it was Tamsyn at the door. Knowing this, she very carefully placed her rolling pin on the side in no great hurry before answering Tamsyn.

'Hello! Are you still up for a jaunt to the seaside?' Tamsyn asked when Cecilia opened the door to her.

'I forgot. I forgot all about our plans. That's most silly of me. Sorry, Tamsyn,' Cecilia admitted.

'Did your meeting with Conner go *that* badly?' Tamsyn asked.

The conversation that Cecilia knew was coming up was not one she wanted to have on the doorstep. She wasn't entirely sure she wanted to have the conversation at all, it was so embarrassing. As she hoped sharing might make her feel better and Tamsyn wasn't usually one to judge, Cecilia decided she would tell Tamsyn what was on her mind.

'I'll tell you inside. I don't feel like going to the seaside. I don't even feel like leaving these four walls today,' Cecilia replied.

'We all get days like that,' Tamsyn said, following Cecilia into her home.

When she entered the kitchen, the first thing Tamsyn noticed was the rolling pin on the side.

'Oh, you were going to bake, weren't you? Do you want me to go?' Tamsyn asked.

'No, Tamsyn. I want the company, as long as you don't mind. I won't be bright and cheery, but I promise to compensate you for your time with fresh scones,' Cecilia replied.

While Cecilia put the rolling pin away and knocked together some scones, which including cooking took her less than half an hour, she told Tamsyn about playing snooker with Conner. Tamsyn didn't speak, but she frowned and scoffed in all the right places.

When Cecilia went on to tell Tamsyn that she went on a date with Jude to get away from Conner, the Cornish girl raised an eyebrow.

'I did wonder if he was interested in you. Usually, I find it hard to tell, but he made it pretty obvious. I bet he loved dating you,' Tamsyn said.

'Well, I'm not sure about that,' Cecilia replied.

'Why not? What happened on the date?' Tamsyn asked.

As Tamsyn's best friend, Cecilia knew she was only asking about the date to be nice. Because of this, she made sure to only mention what was relevant.

'Jude called me Cici. It hit me so hard that I cried, right there in the restaurant. I couldn't even tell him what was wrong. I simply left a couple of notes and ran. It was most embarrassing, and even though I know it's silly, I still haven't got over it, hence the baking,' Cecilia revealed.

The good thing about friendships like the one between Cecilia and Tamsyn was that most things didn't need explaining. Cecilia didn't have to tell Tamsyn why it hurt so much to be called Cici, which was just as well, for she didn't feel up to explaining it.

'Grief isn't something to get over. It's something to live with, and you *do* live with it. I'm not surprised it upset you so much,' Tamsyn replied.

'Thank you, Tamsyn. It's nice that *you* understand, but I know most people don't think that way. What must Jude think?' Cecilia questioned.

At that point, a timer went off to say the scones could come out of the oven. This gave Tamsyn a moment to contemplate what Jude would think.

'Either he'll be kind and understanding or he won't. Whichever it is, there's no problem. If he's nice about it then you can move on. If he isn't nice, why does it matter what he thinks?' Tamsyn said.

As usual, what Tamsyn said made perfect sense to Cecilia.

The scones Cecilia had made were baked to perfection. This was confirmed by the look on Tamsyn's face when she took her first bite. For Cecilia, the best part of baking was giving the results to appreciative friends and family.

For a few minutes, conversation ceased while Cecilia and Tamsyn scoffed scones.

It was Cecilia who broke the silence by saying: 'I need to see Jude again, if only to explain myself or perhaps to offer to go on another date. I don't have his number, but it occurs to me that he's been at the snooker club on the same day, at the same time, three weeks in a row, so I could probably find him there and talk to him.'

'Well, that's up to you,' Tamsyn replied.

'Yes. I'm going to offer him an apology and another chance, if he wants it. But where to go?' Cecilia questioned, thinking out loud.

Tamsyn said nothing, for she had nothing to say.

'Could I take him to the seaside? I know that was supposed to be our thing, but I could take him somewhere we don't go. It would make for a much more casual atmosphere,' Cecilia asked, now expecting a response.

'I couldn't say. For all I know, that's an incredibly romantic idea. All I can tell you is I wouldn't mind. I don't need to be the only person you go to the beach with,' Tamsyn replied.

For a moment, Cecilia had forgotten who she was speaking to. 'I'm sorry, Tamsyn,' she said.

'You don't need to be sorry. It doesn't bother me. I just have nothing to offer. Talking to me about dating is like me talking to you about intravenous cannulation. You can understand the principal, but you don't know what it feels like to experience it. Although, of course, you could learn to do it, and then you'd know, but I can't learn what love feels like,' Tamsyn replied.

Relief washed over Cecilia when she was sure she hadn't upset Tamsyn. She made up her mind on how to proceed with Jude, and that too gave her relief.

*

CHAPTER EIGHT

Cecilia was sat in her car with the key in the ignition from five minutes *before* Jude was due to meet her until twenty minutes *after* he was supposed to have turned up.

'You would not *believe* how busy town is today! Honestly! I just wanted two bits, and it took me ages,' Jude said when he got into Cecilia's Mini Cooper, twenty-five minutes after she had.

'I *would* believe it, for you are late,' Cecilia pointed out.

Jude frowned. 'Oh, nice to see you again too(!)' he replied sarcastically.

Now Cecilia was the one frowning, though Jude couldn't see that for she had her head in her hands. 'Sorry, Jude! I'm supposed to be making it up to you that I walked out on you, and look how I've started! I hope you'll forgive me,' she said.

The frown on Jude's face turned upside down. 'Hey, chillax Ci... Cecilia! I were only joshing with you! I really ought to stop doing that, but I can't help myself. It's like an illness,' he told Cecilia.

'Oh, thank goodness! I thought I'd upset you for a moment there!' Cecilia cried.

'Nah, I were just being my usual stupid self. I'm glad you mentioned our last date though, cos you left something behind that I've brought along to give back to you,' Jude said.

For a few panicky moments, Cecilia ran through her list of belongings in an attempt to work out what she'd left behind. She didn't remember leaving anything, and she hadn't noticed that anything was missing. The panic ended when Jude produced two £20 notes.

'They were for you, to pay for dinner. You were supposed to keep them,' Cecilia said.

'I said *I'd* pay for dinner,' Jude reminded Cecilia.

'Yes you did, but that was before I walked out on you. It hardly seems fair for you to have to pay for my food when I didn't even have the decency to stay to eat it,' Cecilia replied.

Jude shook his head. 'Something I said upset you, which is the reason you left. I have no idea what, but whatever it were, I doubt it were your fault it upset you.

I'd have paid if you stayed, so it ain't different cos you left, so take the money ,' he said .

In response to Jude shaking his head and being insistent, Cecilia shook *her* head and was *insistent*. 'I couldn't possibly take it. I don't want you to pay for a meal that wasn't eaten,' she argued.

'Actually, that meal were eaten. I ate it. It weren't that nice though, so if you insist on paying for it, then I guess I'll let you,' Jude conceded.

Having given in, Jude put the notes back in his pocket and clipped his seatbelt on.

The car started the first time Cecilia turned the key. After glancing across at Jude to check he had his belt on, she put the car in gear and smoothly pulled off her brick driveway.

-

It was only when she joined the fast-moving A120 duel-carriageway that Cecilia realised she'd forgotten something.

'I'd usually have music on. It helps me drive. I forgot to bring a CD with me today though,' Cecilia said, sharing her realisation.

'You could put the radio on, or rather, *I* could put the radio on, as you're driving at seventy,' Jude pointed out.

There was a reason why Cecilia didn't listen to the radio. A reason she didn't necessarily want to share. She couldn't think of a good enough lie though, and Jude needed an answer.

'I don't listen to the radio in the car in case it plays a song I used to listen to with my late mother. I can't have an episode like I had with you in the restaurant when I'm behind the wheel,' Cecilia explained.

Ever since Cecilia had walked out, Jude had wondered why it bothered her so much to be called Cici. He had assumed it was because of a bad ex-boyfriend. Now he assumed, correctly, that it was because that was what her mum used to call her.

'Nah, totally. I'm sorry it happened in the restaurant. I'd be even more sorry if it happened now,' Jude said. He felt the need to add something, so he did. 'Not cos it's wrong to get all teary, you understand. I'm one of those lucky gits who ain't lost anyone, but I hear it's painful, sometimes even physically, and it's a big thing,' he clarified.

For a while, the only noise in the car was from the engine, and the road.

The lull in conversation was broken when Cecilia sighed loudly. 'There's nothing I can do about it, but I'm really cross with myself for not picking up a CD. *Meet The Vamps* is on the side in the hallway, and I just left it sitting there,' she said.

'Did you ever listen to Mika with your mum?' Jude asked.

'No, I don't think I've ever listened to Mika. *She* certainly hasn't. I mean *didn't*,' Cecilia replied.

'One of the things I bought today were *Life In Cartoon Motion*, his debut album. It's one of my all-time faves, but I couldn't find my copy, so I got myself another from one of the second-hand shops. It's in my bag on the back seat. I could pop it in, if you don't mind?' Jude offered.

The thought of having something to listen to that wouldn't make her cry made Cecilia smile. 'I wouldn't mind at all. I really want music to drive to, and it'll be interesting to listen to music you like,' she said.

A minute later, *Grace Kelly* played through Cecilia's Mini's sound system at a sensible volume.

'Wow! What a falsetto!' Cecilia cried when the song got to the chorus.

'Yup. Quite something, ain't it? I quite like the lyrics too. I think they're supposed to be about accepting yourself, and other people, for who they are. Something like that, anyway,' Jude replied.

'An important message. One people, including myself, too often forget,' Cecilia commented.

As he didn't believe he had anything clever to say to that, Jude kept his mouth shut.

After *Grace Kelly* came *Lollipop*, and when the bright and bizarre song started, the smile that Cecilia had had ever since Jude had suggested playing *Life In Cartoon Motion* widened.

'This is *brilliant*! Strange, but so cheerful. Happy music is the best music,' Cecilia enthused. Then her smile morphed into a frown. 'I mean in *my* opinion. I'm not saying there's anything wrong with sombre music. It has its place,' she said.

Jude didn't notice Cecilia's frown. He was too busy enjoying sharing his absolute favourite album with someone who liked it. 'Each to their own, I guess, but I think happy music is best too, especially slightly strange happy music, like this is. The video for this is something else. Even better than the song,' he told Cecilia.

-

For the rest of their journey, Jude and Cecilia listened to slightly strange happy music. It was the best music for their drive to Frinton-On-Sea.

Most of the spaces along the Esplanade were taken, but Cecilia found an empty one and slotted her car into it.

'Good job you've got a Mini,' Jude said as he eased out of the door he could barely open.

'Sorry. Spaces are tight around here. The beach here is nice and peaceful out of season, but I didn't think about how hard it would be to get your door open,' Cecilia replied.

Jude shrugged. 'Looks cool. Feels actually cool with the sea breeze,' he commented.

-

Cecilia lead Jude onto the beach, which was conveniently located just a minute's walk from where she'd parked. Jude was wearing trainers, so couldn't feel the soft and clean sand. As she was wearing sandals, Cecilia could. It was warm, thanks to the sun beating down on it, and it tickled her toes.

'Ah, I forgot how good beaches smell,' Jude said after inhaling deeply.

Until Jude mentioned it, Cecilia hadn't noticed the smell of the beach. It was energising and salty. To her nose, it wasn't entirely pleasant. She didn't say so though. Jude was so enamoured with it that Cecilia assumed she was the only person in the world who didn't like it.

Walking on a beach takes some effort, because your feet sink into the sand with every step, but not so much effort that you can't talk. This is especially true if you trundle along the dunes at no great pace, as Jude and Cecilia did.

'You know, this is a great choice for a date. Is this how you always do dates?' Jude asked.

'No, not at all. This is the first date I've had outside of a restaurant. I'm glad you like it,' Cecilia replied.

'Restaurants can be so stuffy. When the only attraction is food, I feel like I'm supposed to perform in some way. Don't get me wrong, I'm a confident guy, but I'm no performer. I can't entertain a girl for two hours or whatever. This is much better. More casual,' Jude said.

Often, Cecilia felt like she was the only person to think and feel certain things. Things that made perfect sense to her but judging by their behaviour, not to other people. Occasionally, someone said something that reassured her she wasn't alone in some of her opinions and reactions.

'So it's not just me who feels under pressure on dinner dates?' Cecilia asked.

'Nah! As far as I know, loads of people get nervy on formal dates. I mean, if they didn't, *First Dates* would be a really boring show, wouldn't it? No-one would watch it if everyone on it strolled in cool as a courgette. That'd be no fun. Of course, part of the nervousness is just about dating, but I do think the restaurant atmosphere makes it worse,' Jude replied.

Part of Jude's answer surprised Cecilia. 'You watch *First Dates*? The Channel Four show with the dishy French maître d'?' she questioned.

Jude blushed. 'Yup, I do. My housemate puts it on every week, and he loves it. He loves anything romantic. He watches them films you call chick flicks, he reads romances, and when he has a partner for Valentine's, he does the whole dozen red roses and heart-shaped chocolates thing,' he told Cecilia.

To her surprise, Cecilia found herself laughing. Not a quiet little titter, but an unrestrained guffaw. 'Now *that* makes sense! I can picture you moaning when it comes on and sitting down with a great deal of huffing and puffing, only to find yourself completely absorbed within ten minutes,' she said.

'That is what happens! I don't know how, but it does! Floyd pops it on, I tell him and myself that I'll go to bed in a minute, but I never do,' Jude replied, making great big gestures with his hands.

When the laughter faded, silence fell. Not for long though, as Jude didn't want it to be quiet.

'I assume you too watch *First Dates*, but because you want to?' Jude said. Then he tutted and pretended to hit himself on the head. 'Nope, because I should never assume anything. I'll ask instead. Have you watched it?' he asked.

'You listened!' Cecilia cried.

'That's what you're supposed to do when someone talks, ain't it?' Jude replied.

Although she knew that people were supposed to listen when talked to, so many people failed to listen properly that it surprised Cecilia when they did.

To prove that *she* had listened properly, Cecilia answered Jude's question. 'My friend watches it, and she talks about it all the time. You can tell it's not me who watches it. I'd never describe anyone as dishy. She'd probably like your housemate. Her boyfriend never makes big gestures. I know this, as she complains about it almost every time we meet,' she told him.

'She might like *Floyd* then, but she'd hate *me*. I never think to do things like that,' Jude said.

'I never *like* things like that. They're tacky, they're usually expensive, and often they're thoughtless. Surely, it's far better to buy someone a bouquet of their favourite flowers than a cliché bunch of twelve roses, unless their favourite flower *is* the rose,' Cecilia replied.

As if they were agreeing with Cecilia, the gulls flying above her head cawed in unison.

Cecilia stared up at the sky. 'Is it only me, or is that weird?' she asked.

'Nah, it is weird. Just because there's a pretty sign above something or fancy-pants marketing with love hearts, people decide that something is romantic. That's weird,' Jude agreed.

Unbeknownst to Jude, Cecilia had been referring to the gulls crying together, as if coordinated. He never found out about his mistake, for Cecilia didn't mention it.

When Cecilia had first planned the date, she had intended to walk along the beach with Jude and then drive back home. Now she was on the date, her stomach was requesting an amendment to that plan. She accepted the requested amendment because much to her surprise, she was enjoying spending time with Jude, and she believed Jude was enjoying spending time with her.

'Once we've walked up and down the sand, would you like to get fish and chips? I promise not to walk away without even eating my food this time,' Cecilia suggested.

When Cecilia had first made arrangements with Jude for their date, he had expected a stroll along the sands that would last an hour if he was lucky, after which he'd be whisked off back to Colchester. Much to his surprise, this wasn't to be the case, and the prospect of spending bonus time with Cecilia delighted him.

'Sounds cool,' Jude agreed.

*

CHAPTER NINE

As she so often did when she met Cecilia, or anyone but her clients for that matter, Emma-Leigh had shopping bags in her hands. They clunked against the glass door of Trinity Café as she struggled to get through it.

Before even saying a word to Cecilia, Emma-Leigh took a sip of the iced mocha frappé that was waiting for her on the table. Then, and only then, did she flop down in the tub chair opposite Cecilia.

'Ta very much for that. I needed it,' Emma-Leigh said to the friend she'd kept waiting for half an hour.

'Did you?' Cecilia asked. A part of her wanted to say: "Yes, it's thirsty work traipsing round Fenwicks, isn't it(?) Almost as thirst-inducing as waiting thirty minutes for your friend to turn up". She did not say this, for she wished to avoid having to listen to the ear-splitting shriek of indignation Emma-Leigh emitted when offended.

'One hundred percent! You should have *seen* Lauren's kitchen! I don't know what sauce that woman made, but I *do* know the floor she spilt it on *loved* it! It really didn't want to let me clean it off,' Emma-Leigh replied.

Cecilia shook her head. 'Some people, eh?' she commented.

There was a purpose to Cecilia and Emma-Leigh's meeting over coffee. That purpose was discussing Cecilia's recent date with Jude.

'Let's get down to it. How was your pleasant little stroll along the sand with Jude? Give me the full kiss-and-tell,' Emma-Leigh demanded.

'There is no kiss to tell you about, but I can happily say that the date went far better than I expected. It ended up being a bit more than just a walk on the beach. I felt hungry, so we bought fish and chips,' Cecilia replied.

When Cecilia revealed she hadn't kissed Jude, Emma-Leigh frowned. When she went on to say she'd shared an unplanned takeaway with him, Emma-Leigh grinned.

'Did you just extend the date because you were hungry for fish and chips or was there more to it than that?' Emma-Leigh asked.

That was the same question that Cecilia had asked herself while walking down the narrow streets of Frinton with Jude to the fish and chip shop. The conclusion she'd come to surprised her. She suspected it would surprise Emma-Leigh too.

'There was more to it. I was enjoying myself. *Specifically*, I was enjoying Jude's company,' Cecilia revealed.

Emma-Leigh raised an eyebrow. 'Oh, *really*? Tell me more, tell me more! Did he charm you?' she asked.

'I wouldn't say *that*. I found we have a lot in common, which was nice, but that's not why I enjoyed his company. He put me at ease somehow, which was brilliant. He is so easy to be around. It helped that I was by the sea. Tamsyn once told me that the sound of waves is relaxing. Apparently, because of this, she did a lot of her homework sitting on the beach when she was doing her A-levels,' Cecilia told Emma-Leigh.

'So would *I* if I'd been lucky enough to grow up in Cornwall,' Emma-Leigh replied.

In Cecilia's opinion, Tamsyn *hadn't* been lucky to grow up in Cornwall. It wasn't necessary to correct Emma-Leigh though, so she didn't. Instead, she carried on talking about Jude.

'On the whole date, Jude only did two things to annoy me,' Cecilia said.

The only thing Emma-Leigh or indeed most people could say to this was: 'What were they?'

'He turned up late, which always bothers me,' Cecilia revealed, watching Emma-Leigh's reaction closely.

'What was the other thing?' Emma-Leigh asked, her cheeks their usual pale shade of pink and her gaze fixed on Cecilia.

In her mind, though not out loud, Cecilia chuckled to herself.

'The second thing is that Jude tried to give me back the money I dropped on the table when I walked out of the steakhouse. We argued about it, and I convinced him to keep it. I thought I'd won, but just before he left me, he handed the notes to me and said: "This is for petrol". I didn't want to disturb my calm state-of-mind by arguing, so I now have that money again,' Cecilia replied.

Emma-Leigh tutted. 'How ghastly of him(!)' she remarked sarcastically.

'I know it wouldn't bother anyone else, but it bothered me,' Cecilia told Emma-Leigh.

As she sealed her lips around the paper straw sticking out of her frappé, a question came to Emma-Leigh. A question she would ask Cecilia, but not before she'd drained half her cup and given herself brain freeze.

'You said you didn't kiss Jude. Did you *want* to?' Emma-Leigh asked.

'Maybe,' Cecilia answered, smiling at her drink.

*

CHAPTER TEN

As he walked through the door of the mid-terrace house he shared with Floyd, Jude heard the pings and bleeps of a video game coming from the front room. Upon entering the front room, Jude found exactly what he expected to find. Floyd was sitting on the sofa with a white remote in his hand, which he was using to control a pixellated kart on the screen of the telly that sat in one corner of the room.

'Booyah!' Floyd cried as his pixellated kart crossed the pixellated finish line before all the other pixellated karts.

When he saw Jude standing in the doorway, smiling at him, Floyd cleared his throat. 'Um, hi. You okay?' he asked.

'Yup. Don't need to ask you the same question. I think you answered it a few seconds ago,' Jude replied.

A wide grin spread across Floyd's face. 'Suppose I like Mario Kart a bit too much for a twenty-four-year-old man,' he said.

'No such thing. You're fine, mate,' Jude replied.

Floyd looked his friend and housemate up and down and smiled. 'Someone's sunny. Your date went well, methinks. I'd have asked about it yesterday, but instead I was asking: "Would you like the latest Samsung Blah-be-blah X Eight for three times what you're currently paying?",' he told Jude.

'The answer to that is still no. I'm perfectly happy with my Alcatel Thingy A One Three Three,' Jude answered.

'I thought she was called Cecilia?' Floyd questioned.

'I were joking about the phone thing cos you mentioned your job,' Jude explained.

'And I was referring to your recent date because I'm your friend and it's a serious life event. I want to know if you've met the one,' Floyd replied.

Of course, Jude knew Floyd had been talking about his date, just as Floyd knew Jude was joking about his job. As Jude was so flippant, if you wanted to have a serious conversation with him, you had to spell out exactly what you meant and call out his jokes. Floyd had lived with Jude more than long enough to know this. It was lucky that he didn't have to have many serious conversations with him. When he did, he found them exhausting.

"The one" was a concept that was central to Floyd's belief system and the way he lived his life. Some people, such as Jude, don't believe in "the one", and live their lives accordingly.

Even though he didn't believe in "the one", Jude knew Cecilia was special. He believed she was: "the something".

'The date went well. More well than I thought it would. I didn't make any major gaffs, and she seemed to like it. I mean, she must have done, cos she's challenged me to arrange another date for us,' Jude told Floyd.

'Yes, mate! This is *good*!' Floyd cried.

Now he knew Cecilia was going to be a part of his friend and housemate's life, Floyd's interest was piqued further. In order to make an educated guess at how long Cecilia would be a part of Jude's life, Floyd decided to ask him a few questions about what had attracted him to her.

'Is she rich?' Floyd asked.

'I dunno. I mean, she owns a car that starts without thinking about it first, a Mini Cooper no less, so she can't be broke. I doubt that she's rich, cos she took me to a beach,' Jude replied.

To Floyd, that was the perfect answer.

'Is she pretty?' Floyd asked.

'Yup. She's a stunner!' Jude answered without hesitation. Then he sighed. 'She don't act like she knows that though. We went to the chippy, and while waiting in there, she said about how pretty it was inside. I said something like: "It is now". She didn't get it. She thought I were going on about a renovation or something. It didn't occur to her that she were the reason it were pretty. Weren't such a nice little compliment when I had to spell it out,' Jude said.

That reply gave Floyd a detailed picture of Cecilia and her character. He had dated girls who, no matter how much affection he lavished on them, couldn't see how special they were. This knowledge made him want to warn Jude to tread carefully. He didn't, because he worried Jude might be offended by such a warning.

In lieu of a warning, Floyd asked one last question, which was: 'Do you see this going somewhere?'

Jude shook his head and replied: 'Nah! A woman like her don't want a guy like me. I know that from experience. I'm gonna enjoy it while it lasts, but she ain't gonna stay with me.'

*

CHAPTER ELEVEN

The Colneside Entertainment Centre, a large concrete rectangle that sat next to the River Colne, was home to an arcade, a bowling alley, a steakhouse, a coffee shop, and a snooker club. Jude intended to make use of only one of the aforementioned facilities on his date with Cecilia.

'What made you choose this for our date?' Cecilia asked when she located Jude at the time agreed, in the place agreed.

There were a few reasons why Jude had chosen the activity that he had. The main one was that during the day, it was reasonably affordable. The one he chose to tell Cecilia was: 'You didn't seem to enjoy it when you played it before.'

'You're right that I don't enjoy snooker. Surely that means it's a terrible choice for a date. Unless, of course, you don't like me, in which case I'd rather you simply told me that,' Cecilia replied.

'Nah, I like you, Cecilia. That's why I'm doing this,' Jude answered swiftly. After clearing his throat, he went on to explain why he'd chosen an activity Cecilia didn't like. 'Morton and your ginger friend showed you how to play well, but they didn't show you how to play for fun. That's what I'd like to do. I want to show you how to enjoy this,' Jude explained.

'I understand now. Can you do that? Can you play to a poor standard and still enjoy it?' Cecilia asked.

Jude chuckled. 'Morton would say you can't, but as I lose to him almost every week and still have a great time, I think otherwise,' he replied.

Now that she understood it, Cecilia quite liked Jude's idea. As she watched him set the table up, she wondered what the trick was to having fun; not just fun in snooker, but in general.

With the natural lack of concentration Cecilia had come to expect from Jude, he played a break-off shot that sent the cue ball careering into the blue on its way back to the safety of the baulk end. This was a common mistake that many snooker players made.

In the few seconds it took her to walk to the table, Cecilia spotted a red which had drifted away from the mostly-unbroken pack into what might be a pottable position. She'd have to hit it exactly right with the cue ball, but it could be done.

When Cecilia got down on her shot, which was aimed to glance off the pack to send the cue ball to safety, Jude decided to question her choice. 'I thought I saw you look at the red to the left,' he said.

'I'd probably miss it though,' Cecilia replied.

'Don't you wanna find out? It'd be cool if it came off,' Jude suggested.

Cecilia did want to find out. She stood up and then got down again in position for the first shot she'd spotted. After taking a deep breath, she struck the cue ball perfectly, sending the red straight into the pocket, just where she wanted it.

The surprise of seeing the red ball disappear made Cecilia squeal. 'I did it! I did that!' she cried.

'And that's how you have fun,' Jude said with a smile.

In snooker, after potting a red ball, you must hit a colour ball. If you pot that, it goes back on the table and you must hit another red ball. If you pot that, the cycle continues until you miss, or all the red balls are gone, when you then move onto the colours, which are to be potted in ascending order.

Buoyed with confidence, Cecilia took aim at a distant blue. When hit towards the pocket, it bounced around in the jaws, but was too stubborn to fall. This broke the cycle, ended Cecilia's turn at the table, and shattered her confidence.

'Oh, I thought I was good for a second,' Cecilia said.

Jude chuckled. 'You are. It's just that this is a tricky game. Not everything can work. One mistake don't make you not good at something, ' he told Cecilia.

'I guess not,' Cecilia answered.

-

Though he was not normally a good player, Jude managed to pot several balls in a row off the back of Cecilia's missed blue. This stunned him so much, it rendered him speechless.

Just as Cecilia was wondering if it would be rude to get her phone out, Jude missed an adventurous double.

'Oh, I can't believe it! I got so absorbed in what I were doing that I just totally blanked you! Sorry, Cecilia!' Jude cried when he remembered he was on a date.

When she'd been sitting in her uncomfortable seat, waiting for a turn or some attention, Cecilia had felt irritated. Now Jude had apologised for ignoring her, she found his absent-mindedness adorable. She also found it quite attractive.

'I did wonder if you'd forgotten me,' Cecilia said with a smile.

'I had. I totally had! What with how pretty you are, I wouldn't have thought it possible to forget about you, but obviously it was,' Jude replied.

'Do you think you can dig yourself out of it by complimenting me?' Cecilia asked.

'Nah, you actually are pretty, and I'm so sorry for blanking you. I mean it. I dunno how to make it up to you,' Jude told Cecilia.

The deep lines that had appeared on Jude's forehead, combined with his newfound inability to look at her, amused Cecilia. It also appealed to her.

'I'll forgive you because you're *adorable*. The expression you're pulling right now is most cute,' Cecilia replied.

'You think I'm cute?' Jude questioned.

Now Cecilia was the one who was embarrassed. She hadn't intended to reveal to Jude how attracted she was to him. 'Maybe I do,' she told him, gazing at the floor.

'Now who's the cute one, Little Miss Can't Look At Me Cos I'm So Cute?' Jude asked.

A little titter escaped Cecilia, but she found she couldn't answer.

'May I suggest that we both agree that we're both cute?' Jude said.

Cecilia nodded.

'I, Jude Austen , do solemnly swear that you, Cecilia Whatever-your-surname-is, is cute,' Jude declared.

'If you're imitating wedding vows, then you should have said your full name, including any middle names you might have,' Cecilia pointed out.

'Thanks. I'll remember that next time I make a wedding vow related joke,' Jude replied.

A moment later, Jude and Cecilia burst out laughing.

-

The pair laughed many more times while at the snooker club. Mostly when Jude's increasingly ambitious shots were unsuccessful. One time, they laughed in astonishment when Cecilia made a four-ball plant.

Laughter releases endorphins, reduces stress hormones, and relaxes the muscles. That was partly why Cecilia felt so light when she descended The Colneside's main staircase. Her feeling of weightlessness was also thanks to the presence of the man who had made her laugh. It had been a long time since she'd felt that good.

*

CHAPTER TWELVE

'Hope this ain't too fancy for you,' Jude said to Cecilia as he lead her into a chain burger joint.

'I've always wanted to come here, but I always seem to end up in McDonald's instead!' Cecilia cried.

The excitement in Cecilia's voice made Jude smile.

As Colchester has a large student population, the burger joint was busy. There was a long queue to the counter, which made the long and narrow restaurant feel crowded. A young man passing the queue with his brown paper bag of yummy-smelling food bumped into Cecilia, causing her to brush against Jude's arm. For the brief second she was in contact with Jude, Cecilia felt a rush of heat through her body.

'What a jerk! Are you okay?' Jude asked Cecilia.

'I think so,' Cecilia murmured.

-

Once they had their food, Jude and Cecilia took a seat at the only available table. The food was in two separate bags. Jude handed the one containing Cecilia's bacon double cheeseburger to her, brushing her eagerly outstretched hand in the process. Instead of taking her bag and letting Jude go, Cecilia grasped his hand and looked straight into his grey eyes.

'Jude, I feel something for you that I haven't felt in ages,' Cecilia told him. The words, and the accompanying squeeze of Jude's slightly gnarled hand, were completely unplanned. They just happened. Her inhibitions seemed to have abandoned her, as if she'd been drinking prosecco. She had actually been drinking diet lemonade. She was feeling dreamy, not drunk.

'I get it,' Jude replied.

Without another word, Jude leaned across the table and planted his lips on Cecilia's. The abrupt and unromantic nature of this action made Cecilia laugh, so he immediately withdrew before he was able to fully appreciate how soft her lips were.

Suddenly, Cecilia felt a dramatic but familiar personality shift occur in her mind.

'That's not how you do it!' Cecilia complained.

'It ain't, is it? Sorry,' Jude replied.

Cecilia scoffed and tapped the padded bench she was sitting on. 'Let me show you how to do it properly,' she ordered.

There was no arguing with Cecilia. Her tone and fixed expression made that clear. Not that Jude really wanted to argue. The idea of being close to Cecilia set his pulse racing.

Once Jude was sat next to her, Cecilia slipped her right arm around him and angled her body towards his ever so slightly. She could hear his unsteady breathing, which betrayed his excitement.

'First, you get close to your partner,' Cecilia said, gently stroking Jude's right arm with her left hand.

'Yup. Closeness is a good start,' Jude agreed.

Following her natural instincts, Cecilia brought her face tantalisingly close to Jude's. Close enough for him to feel her warm breath on his lips.

'Next, you get closer still,' Cecilia murmured.

'Got that,' Jude replied.

The hand Cecilia had been using to stroke Jude's arm came up to encourage his head to tilt slightly to the right.

'Then, you angle your head,' Cecilia whispered.

'Of course,' Jude uttered.

Having used it to angle Jude's head, Cecilia ran her left hand through his curly brown hair to his crown. She then closed her eyes, and closed the distance between her lips and Jude's to zero. The moment her lips met Jude's, Cecilia felt pleasure flood through her. It wasn't just her sense of touch that was engaged. For the first time, she noticed that Jude was wearing a subtle woody aftershave. The multi-sensory stimuli sent a wave of tingly heat traveling through her body. She let it reach her fingers and toes, and then broke the connection.

The look in Jude's eyes was the one Cecilia wanted to see; shock.

'That, Jude, is how you kiss,' Cecilia told him.

'Uh-huh,' Jude agreed.

All of a sudden, the personality shift was reversed. Cecilia became aware of the many sets of eyes watching her and Jude. She blushed, and scooched down the bench, away from Jude.

'I forgot where I was. Lia took over. I'm so sorry for making a scene,' Cecilia said.

Sensing Cecilia's awkwardness, Jude got up and moved back to his seat.

'Kissing like that, I'm not surprised you forgot where you was. I totally did. Ain't that a good thing?' Jude questioned.

'Not when half the town is watching,' Cecilia replied.

Jude just about managed to stop himself saying: "Who cares?". He knew the answer would have been: "Me". Instead he said: 'It's all in takeaway bags. We could find ourselves a bench somewhere.'

'Please can we do that? Now?' Cecilia practically begged.

The pair were followed by seven pairs of eyes as they walked out of the burger joint.

Out on the High Street, a breeze was blowing between the buildings, but it didn't cool Jude or Cecilia.

*

CHAPTER THIRTEEN

Putting her uniform on made Tamsyn feel she was prepared for anything. The green fabric of the clothes couldn't help her handle the variety of challenges she faced on placements, but it reminded her of all the people wearing similar outfits who *could* help her. One day, if everything went to plan, she'd earn the right to fully be one of them.

The fridge in the kitchen Tamsyn shared with three other medical students had a full length mirror next to it. One of her housemates had said this would help prevent overeating. The housemate had failed to explain how the mirror would prevent overeating. That didn't matter to Tamsyn though, for she only used the mirror to check she was presentable.

While Tamsyn was admiring her green uniform, Scott walked into the kitchen in his pale blue one.

'It looks good on you,' Scott commented.

'I feel so honoured to be allowed to wear it. I feel such a sense of pride when I put this on,' Tamsyn replied.

'I'm like that with this. These clothes represent years of study. I've wanted this for as long as I can remember,' Scott told Tamsyn.

Tamsyn span round to face Scott with a beaming smile on her face. 'I love that you know how it feels. Our uniforms mean so much. They don't *just* represent our education. They don't *just* represent us in general. They represent something much bigger than that. Something we dream of being a part of,' she enthused.

The smile on Tamsyn's face was mirrored on Scott's. 'Couldn't have put it better myself,' he replied.

Having spoken about Tamsyn's uniform, Scott looked it up and down. 'Green is a difficult colour to pull off, but you wear it well. I hope you qualify, because the uniform suits you so well,' he said.

'Same to you,' Tamsyn replied.

'I'm not wearing green. This is blue,' Scott pointed out.

Tamsyn laughed. 'You know what I mean!' she cried.

'Yeah. I think I do,' Scott replied huskily, taking a step closer to Tamsyn.

There was a clock on the kitchen wall, which was glanced at by several people, several times a day, for several different reasons. Tamsyn glanced at it to check if she had to leave; she did.

'I must be off now so I can train for the role I wear this uniform for. Thanks for the chat, and good luck at the hospital,' Tamsyn told Scott.

'I love chatting to you. Good luck on the ambulance, not that you need it,' Scott replied.

–

'You're looking awfully sunny today,' Ian said to Tamsyn when she leapt into the vehicle they were to share for many hours.

'I am. My day started with a phone call from my best friend, who might be in love. That set me up for the day nicely. I then had a chat with my student nurse housemate about how much our uniforms mean to us. Then, after all that, I get to come here and spend time helping the varied people of Essex with the best paramedic in the service. I'm on top of the world,' Tamsyn told her paramedic mentor.

Before answering Tamsyn, Ian waved at his wife, a fellow paramedic mentor, who was in the vehicle next to his. Tamsyn waved too, for thanks to lengthy chats with Ian, she felt like she knew her.

'It's that kind of attitude, my paramedic prodigy, that will one day make you the service's second best paramedic,' Ian said.

'Better than your wife?' Tamsyn questioned.

Ian cackled. 'No! No-one could be better than my Alma. I meant better than me,' he replied.

The compliment both cheered and embarrassed Tamsyn. She blushed and grinned simultaneously. 'It's not possible to be better than you and Alma, but I'd settle for third best. That's my aim: to be the third best paramedic in the service,' she declared.

*

CHAPTER FOURTEEN

The Tower's Shadow, the restaurant Cecilia had chosen for her date with Jude, had stark and formal decor. It appeared to be the sort of place that made them both feel uncomfortable.

'-iya, ducky! You -ere for your table for two in the corner, are you?' the waiter at the lectern asked Cecilia when she walked into his employer's restaurant.

'I am, but I know I'm early. Sorry about that, Rhys. I didn't mean to be. I'll wander around town for a while if you need me to,' Cecilia replied.

Rhys the waiter swished a carefree hand through the air. 'It's fine, it's fine! There's no-one on it anyway, and if there was, I'd chuck –em off fo- you,' he told her.

Cecilia smiled. 'Thank you. I don't want to be any trouble, but I'd love to sit down,' she said.

Once again, Rhys waved casually. 'Please? You couldn't be trouble even if you tried to be, darlin-. Come on, now. Follow me to your table,' he replied.

As she walked through the restaurant, oblivious to all the heads that turned to watch her, Cecilia thought about how vast the contrast was between the menu and decor, and the staff's demeanour. One was frigid and off-putting, while the other was warm and welcoming.

The table Cecilia had requested when she'd visited The Tower's Shadow a few days ago was adorned with small plastic fake diamonds that surrounded a cream tealight, which was sitting on a frosted glass saucer.

'Isn'- it fabulous?' Rhys asked.

'Totally fabulous, and romantic in an understated way. You've done a great job for me. This'll be great. Thank you,' Cecilia said.

Rhys beamed. 'I'm thrilled! I did hope you'd like it,' he replied.

From the wooden chair she sat down on, Cecilia could see the entrance, so she'd be able to see Jude arrive. She could also see a family of diners waiting by the lectern, as could Rhys.

'Oh, I'm n-glecting my du-ies! I must dash!' Rhys cried.

The waiter minced off to the entrance, leaving Cecilia alone with her thoughts.

When planning the date, Cecilia had deliberately scheduled in some time alone at the table so she could get herself in the right frame of mind. It was easy to arrange. All she'd done was tell Jude to arrive at a time that was fifteen minutes later than the time she'd booked the table for.

It was a very particular frame of mind that Cecilia wanted to get herself into; the frame of mind that had overcome her when she'd kissed Jude. Thanks to turning up early, she now had twenty-six minutes to transform herself into a different person; a person she called Lia.

-

Thirty minutes later, neither Jude nor Lia had turned up, but several people Cecilia didn't know *had*. The tables around her were filling up fast.

To keep herself entertained, Cecilia was reading a proof copy of a book that didn't contain any errors, but *did* contain compelling characters. It wasn't in her job description to enjoy the books she checked for errors, but she couldn't help it sometimes.

Footsteps approached Cecilia. She looked up, expecting to see Jude, and saw Rhys the waiter instead.

'I do apologise for not comin- to see you soone-. It's been chocka in -ere,' Rhys told Cecilia. It was then that he noticed the empty chair opposite her. 'Have they not turned up yet?' he asked.

'No, he hasn't. He hasn't text me to say he's not coming either. He was late for the last date I organised, but not quite this late. I'm getting worried,' Cecilia replied.

'Oh, don't worry, ducky! I'm sure he's fine,' Rhys said.

Cecilia shook her head. 'That's not what I'm worried about. I kissed him on the last date, and now I'm wondering if I scared him off,' she told the waiter.

This revelation made Rhys frown, so for a moment Cecilia worried that he too thought she'd scared Jude. 'I doub- it. I-'ll jus- be that he's lost track of time or some-hing like that,' Rhys replied, allaying Cecilia's fears slightly.

There then fell silence. Cecilia didn't know what to say. She was sinking into her own little world, and it wasn't a happy or chatty world.

'Can I get you anythin-?' Rhys asked Cecilia. The question was the reason he'd visited her table, but he'd forgotten all about it when he'd realised she was still alone. It was only the silence, which he found awkward, that reminded him he had a job to do.

'I'd love a glass of prosecco, please. It might help settle me a bit,' Cecilia replied.

'Then a glass of prosecco you shall -ave,' Rhys told Cecilia. He then waltzed off to get it.

-

The prosecco didn't last very long, and it didn't help very much. Prosecco was a popular choice at The Tower's Shadow. Many women at the tables near Cecilia were drinking it. While they drank it, some of the diners muttered to each other about Cecilia, sitting all alone at a table that was obviously set up for a date. Cecilia couldn't hear their words, but she caught their pitying glances and discreet nods in her direction.

As time passed, and more people discussed her, Cecilia felt heavier and heavier. It was the exact opposite of what had happened on her last date with Jude. In her solitude, Cecilia mused that mood was like ice cream. When it was warm, you could cut through it easily, and it felt light and airy. When it was cold, it was a solid and weighty lump that yielded to nothing, except warmth.

'Hey! I totally forgot what day it were until Floyd came home. The moment I realised, I jumped in the shower, threw this on, and came straight here. Not at the same time, obviously. Sorry for being a bit late,' a cheery voice said.

Cecilia looked up from the page she'd been staring at for ten minutes and saw Jude standing before her in a creased checked shirt and dark blue jeans.

'You forgot about me?' Cecilia questioned. She found it hard to speak, and her words came out in a soft whisper.

'I forgot what day it were. *You* are impossible to forget,' Jude replied with a smile.

This time Cecilia found it wasn't hard to speak, but *impossible*.

In the absence of something to reply to, Jude glanced around at his surroundings. 'This seems like the exact sort of place we were talking about on the beach. I thought we agreed we don't like this sort of thing. Didn't I listen properly or something?' he questioned.

'On that occasion, you listened, but this restaurant is more comfortable than it looks, so it's not the type of place we were discussing. You clearly did not listen properly when I told you what time to be here,' Cecilia replied. Suddenly she had found her voice, albeit a quiet one.

'Okay, so I were more than a bit late. I totally am sorry about that,' Jude told Cecilia.

When Jude proceeded to sit down, Cecilia stood up. He gazed up at her, one eyebrow raised.

'You're sorry?! I've spent well over an hour sitting here wondering what I did wrong on our last date, while everyone tittle-tattled about me!' Cecilia cried.

'Tittle-tattled? That is the most middle-class word I've ever heard,' Jude replied.

Cecilia shook her head. 'You don't understand, do you?' she questioned.

After taking a moment to think about it, Jude concluded that he did understand. 'I get it. It's dead boring sitting here by yourself. I'm here now, so let's just sit down and have a nice meal,' he said.

'Jude, I'm in no mood to have a date now. Eighty-three minutes ago, when you were supposed to be here, I was excited and dreaming about how my night might end. Now I'm all flustered in completely the wrong way, and furious with you for being so ridiculously late,' Cecilia replied.

By now, Cecilia's tone was so loud that the diners on the surrounding tables were eavesdropping and making no attempt to hide it. Jude could feel countless pairs of female eyes burning into him.

'Look, I've said I'm sorry. Can you not just sit down and eat with me? You was the one who wanted to eat in this poncy place. I'm sure everything will be okay once you've got a few more glasses of prosecco down you,' Jude said.

By Cecilia's feet was a white leather shoulder bag, which she had brought with her because she was wearing a black evening gown, which did not have pockets. She picked it up and threw the strap over her shoulder so she could open the flap and rummage through the varied contents in search of her purse without having to bend to the floor, which would have been ungainly and uncomfortable. Upon locating her purse, she pulled out a £20 note and slammed it down on the table.

'It's not only that you were late; you were so blasé about it. You could have rescued the situation, but you didn't. You won't be giving this note back, because you'll never see me again,' Cecilia declared.

After a slight pause to allow Jude to respond, which he failed to take, Cecilia stormed through the restaurant.

When Cecilia walked past the lectern by the entrance, Rhys was standing behind it. He, like most people in The Tower's Shadow, had watched and listened to the heated exchange between Jude and Cecilia.

'I've left a twenty pound note on my table. You can keep whatever the change is. It won't be a proper tip, but I'll be back, so I'll make up for it then,' Cecilia told the waiter.

'Oh, darlin-! I'm thrilled that you'll be back, but I'm sorry abou- this visi-,' Rhys replied.

The warmth in Rhys's tone made Cecilia smile. 'It's nice to know someone cares about me, but I don't think you can apologise for Jude's lax attitude,' she said.

'I s-ppose not, but this is the third or fourth date you've had -ere that hasn't worked ou-, so I do feel like we migh- be responsible,' Rhys explained.

'Oh, blame the internet for that, not this place. There's a reason why I gave up on online dating so quickly. Blame snooker clubs too, because that's where I met my now-ex, Jude,' Cecilia replied.

All Cecilia wanted was to get back to the comfort of her little house so she could crawl into bed and pull the covers around herself. That meant she had to end her conversation with the nice waiter, so she smiled at him and said: 'Goodbye.'

As the sound of Cecilia's high block heels pounding the tiled floor filled The Tower's Shadow, Rhys thought: '*What fabulous shoes to storm out in.*'

*

CHAPTER FIFTEEN

Being a student meant Tamsyn didn't have much money, and being a Methodist meant that she didn't drink alcohol, so she didn't go on nights out. The only regular social event in her calendar was pool with Scott. On those nights, she drank tap water or nursed a lemonade, so it didn't cost too much or contravene her religious beliefs.

Most weeks, Tamsyn enjoyed her time with Scott. He was undemanding company, and they both loved the simple yet unpredictable game of pool.

The night after Tamsyn found out Cecilia had dumped Jude, Scott was quiet and insular, which was unlike him. He'd barely said two words to Tamsyn since they'd got to the pub, and his performance on the pool table was far below his usual standard.

'Scott? Is everything alright with you?' Tamsyn asked when he missed a shot by four inches and didn't react at all.

'Yeah. Sorry I'm distant. I've got stuff on my mind,' Scott replied.

'A problem shared is a problem halved. Is it uni work? Final year is so intense, isn't it?' Tamsyn asked.

'It's nothing to do with uni work, but intense is the perfect word for my feelings,' Scott said.

Some people might give up the conversation at this point and carry on with whatever they were doing. Others would directly demand their enigmatic friend open up. There are many individuals who fall between these two options; it is a spectrum. On that spectrum, Tamsyn fell close to one end.

'And what are those feelings? Part of your course is mental health. You know it's important to talk,' Tamsyn said.

'Fine! You asked for this. Remember that,' Scott replied.

Tamsyn nodded.

'I'm in love with you, Tamsyn,' Scott revealed.

The moment Scott said the word "love", Tamsyn felt all traces of happiness leave her. An evening that had simply been dull was about to take a much more serious turn.

'I'm really sorry, but I just don't feel that way,' Tamsyn told Scott.

'Are you sure? We seem so close. Do you see me as a brother? Is that it?' Scott questioned.

It was clear that Scott was desperate for an explanation. That was convenient, because Tamsyn wanted to provide one. Scott was right that they were close, so she felt comfortable to talk to him.

'It's not that, Scott. If you want, we can grab a table, the type you sit at, and I'll explain myself,' Tamsyn offered.

When Scott sullenly agreed, Tamsyn abandoned the pool table mid-game and followed him to one corner of the pub. There, she sat down and revealed one of the few secrets she kept.

*

CHAPTER SIXTEEN

'Are you busy?' Tamsyn asked Cecilia when she answered her phone.

'No, I got through the door five minutes ago. Are you okay?' Cecilia asked in reply.

'Technically yes, but I don't feel alright. I feel like I want to chat to my kind and understanding friend,' Tamsyn told Cecilia.

It was rare that Tamsyn asked Cecilia for anything. Cecilia didn't ask her for much either. It wasn't that sort of friendship. This meant that if one of them asked the other for a favour, the one being asked knew it mattered. A request from Tamsyn was more important to Cecilia than a request from Emma-Leigh.

'I don't mind at all. Is it your parents?' Cecilia asked.

'No, it's Scott, the student nurse I play pool with. Last night, he told me he loves me,' Tamsyn replied.

There was a plush armchair in Cecilia's beloved lounge, which she sank into. She got the feeling this was going to be a long conversation, and she wanted to conduct it in comfort.

'I see. Did you tell him that you can't return his feelings?' Cecilia asked.

'I did. I spent ages explaining myself. The last person I told was you, and that was two years ago, so I'd forgotten how long it takes,' Tamsyn replied.

'It's worth it though, to get it off your chest,' Cecilia said.

For a moment, Tamsyn forgot she was on the phone, so she shook her head. 'It's *not* worth it when they don't believe you. He told me that I was just scared of love. Either that or I hadn't met the right man yet. He basically said it's impossible to feel the way I feel,' she told Cecilia.

Flashbacks of her worst dating app date came to Cecilia. She and Tamsyn weren't the same, not at all, but they'd suffered similar ignorance and prejudice.

'Then this Scott is an idiot. He's not even an *original* idiot, because I've heard that sort of thing before. I've had similar said to me,' Cecilia replied.

'Of course! I forget you're bi sometimes. Sorry about that. Sorry too for calling you to moan when you're not having a good time, what with breaking up with Jude,' Tamsyn said.

Just like Tamsyn, Cecilia momentarily forgot she was on the phone, so she shrugged. 'It's fine. I'm simply glad that I dumped him sooner rather than later. I wouldn't have liked to fall for him any more. The thing that bothers me most about it is that I didn't get to eat in that restaurant. It's such a good restaurant,' she told Tamsyn.

In a flash of inspiration, Cecilia had a great idea. She jumped to her feet and snapped her fingers in excitement.

'Tamsyn, you don't have lectures or placement tomorrow, do you?' Cecilia asked.

'No, I don't, but you probably have work to do. What are you thinking?' Tamsyn answered.

'I'm thinking that you should slip into something nice so I can drive over there and take you out,' Cecilia revealed.

'Oh, Cecilia! You don't have to do that! I just called for a little moan, that's all!' Tamsyn cried.

Cecilia knew she didn't have to take Tamsyn out. She had made the offer because she *wanted* to. She wanted to sit in a lovely restaurant with a lovely woman. Who wouldn't?

'Tamsyn, I adore you. I adore The Tower's Shadow too, and I want to share it with you. Please let me treat you. We both thoroughly deserve it,' Cecilia begged.

As a poor student who didn't date, Tamsyn didn't get to go to nice restaurants. The idea appealed to her. It appealed to her so much that she said: 'Thank you times a million. It'd be my pleasure to spend the evening with you.'

*

CHAPTER SEVENTEEN

'Millie! Hey, what's up?' Jude asked when his sister called him.

It wasn't a convenient time for Jude to talk. He was traversing the Lanes of Colchester in an attempt to find a client he was supposed to meet with. As Millie never called him anymore, he assumed it must be important, so he stopped dead in the street to talk to her. It was lucky that she'd called while he was in a pedestrianised area, otherwise he'd have been in the way of cars, not just irate shoppers.

'I'm pregnant, that's what's up!' Millie cried.

Had Jude not been in public, where there were small children running through town with their parents, he might have sworn. He swore inside his head and had to take several deep breaths before he could think of a clean response to his sister's revelation.

'Have you just found out?' Jude asked. There was no reason for asking this question, except that Jude didn't know what else to say.

'I'm seven days late now. Something must be up,' Millie replied.

'Late? Late for what? I thought you said you were pregnant?' Jude questioned.

'My period, you pillock!' Millie cried.

Periods were not something Jude thought of much, especially his sister's. He was unaware that a change to someone's menstrual cycle can be an indicator of pregnancy. He was also unaware that it can be an indicator of many other things too.

'So you're pregnant then? You've peed on the stick and got two lines or whatever it is you do?' Jude questioned.

There was silence on the line.

'Millie? Are you there?' Jude asked.

'I can't do it. I know I'm pregnant, I must be, but I can't bare to see those two lines. At least not all alone,' Millie replied.

'You could use one of those digital tests. Then it would be words, not lines,' Jude suggested.

A quiet giggle came down the line, and Jude smiled. Millie's laugh hadn't changed in nineteen years, and he loved hearing it.

'You won't be alone, Millie. I'll come to Cambridge, and I'll stand with you when you take that test,' Jude told his sister. It then occurred to him that wasn't exactly what he meant. 'I mean I'll stand with you when you get the result. I really don't wanna watch you pee,' he clarified.

Once again, Millie giggled.

'Thank you, Jude. Thank you so much. I've been so alone. I can't wait to see you,' Millie said.

'Well you won't have to wait long. I'm gonna hang up now, then I'll head straight back home to my car. By the time you go to bed tonight, you'll know,' Jude replied.

After thanking Jude again, Millie let him go.

Once Millie was gone, Jude returned his phone to his jeans pocket and to no-one in particular cried: 'I don't have enough petrol in the stupid car or enough money in the stupid bank to fill the stupid car, and somehow I have to get to stupid Cambridge, where my very intelligent sister is pregnant! This is all just so stupid!'

'Yeah, that does sound stupid. Good luck with it, mate,' a voice said from the floor.

When Jude had been on the phone to Millie, he had forgotten

about his surroundings and the issues of all the people in the square. He had forgotten that there were homeless people on Colchester's streets, like the man who had just spoken to him.

'Oh, mate! I'm here complaining about not having enough money for petrol, and you don't even have enough for a bed for the night. I got no right to moan. I'm sorry, mate,' Jude said to the homeless man.

The homeless man shrugged. 'It's all relative, ain't it? I get it. Everyone has their own issues,' he replied.

'That's nice of you to say, but I really shouldn't moan. Can I get you food or something?' Jude asked.

'I'm never gonna say no to hot food, but ain't you meant to be racing off to stupid Cambridge, in your stupid car, with no stupid petrol?' the homeless man questioned.

In spite of how stressed he was feeling, Jude smiled. 'The petrol weren't stupid, I just don't have enough of it, and I can spare a minute to get you something. It's the least I can do,' he replied.

Having been offered food, the homeless man was now smiling too. 'Cheers, mate. I'd love that. Good luck with everything,' he said.

'I'm gonna need luck,' Jude replied. In his head, he added: *'I'm gonna need all the help I can get, as is Millie.'*

*

CHAPTER EIGHTEEN

Because they met for lunch so often, Cecilia liked to vary where she and Emma-Leigh met. Today, she had picked an independent bakery called The Lion Walk Bakery.

'The pastries look mouth-watering! I can't wait until we've polished off our rolls so we can have one,' Emma-Leigh commented when she sat down with Cecilia.

'Do you have time for dessert? I thought you had a full schedule this afternoon?' Cecilia questioned.

Emma-Leigh shrugged. 'Oh, it'll be fine. I have to do Mr Wight's place today, and he won't mind if I finish late. I've been home early for months now, so my fella shouldn't mind if I'm a bit late tonight,' she replied.

The Lion Walk Bakery offered takeaway and eat-in, and attracted a steady stream of customers for both. Cecilia watched them, and noticed that one of them could not stand still. He kept shifting his weight from foot to foot and glancing at his watch. This was unusual behaviour for the man. Cecilia knew this because she knew the man. It worried her that he was acting so out of character, so she approached him.

'Cecilia! I didn't know you'd be here. I'm sorry. I know you hoped you'd never see me again,' Jude said when Cecilia approached him.

'Colchester isn't *that* big. I knew I'd run into you every now and then. I simply thought I'd ignore you,' Cecilia replied.

'Sounds sensible to me. Why didn't you then? Even if I'd have spotted you in here, I wouldn't have bothered you,' Jude questioned.

'Something's wrong, Jude, and I'm not talking about your behaviour at the restaurant, which was appalling. I'm talking about your behaviour today. You're not okay,' Cecilia said.

On another day, Jude might have tried to be aloof and nonchalant around Cecilia in the hope that would win her back. On that day, Jude didn't feel aloof and nonchalant, and he didn't have the energy to act. This meant he gave into his impulse to tell Cecilia everything about his distressing phone call with Millie.

-

It took Jude a few minutes to relate to Cecilia the details of Millie's, and now his, predicament. She did not interrupt him once. She just listened, and formed a plan in her head.

'You're lucky you ran into me. Me who has a full tank of petrol, a decent knowledge of Cambridge, and a job that doesn't have fixed hours,' Cecilia said when Jude had finished talking.

'What?' Jude questioned.

'I'm going to drive you to Cambridge, that's what,' Cecilia explained.

'For real?' Jude questioned.

'No, I'm going to act out driving to Cambridge(!) ' Cecilia replied sarcastically.

It confused Jude that Cecilia would offer to help him after he'd treated her so badly. It confused him so much that he didn't answer Cecilia, or notice that she'd returned to her table, where Emma-Leigh was waiting.

'I'm sorry, Emma-Leigh, but I need to go. You'll have to eat pastries without me,' Cecilia told her friend.

'Is that Jude?' Emma-Leigh asked.

'Yes it is. He needs me, or rather, his sister does,' Cecilia replied.

'Ooh, exciting! Tell me everything when you get back,' Emma-Leigh said.

'Goodbye, Emma-Leigh,' Cecilia replied, ignoring her friend's request for gossip.

By now, Jude had realised Cecilia had abandoned him. He was hovering by the counter, where he was waiting for a hot soup in a pot, and an Americano in a takeaway cup.

Cecilia rejoined Jude just as his order was given to him by the baker. She grasped his wrist and said: 'Come on! We need to go.'

The only argument Jude made was: 'I need to give this to a homeless man first.'

*

CHAPTER NINETEEN

For most of the ninety minutes of the drive to Cambridge, the only sound in Cecilia's Mini came from her speakers, which were playing one of her favourite albums.

At one point, while the Mini was stuck in traffic on the M11, Jude commented on the music. 'This does sound like something that happened to someone,' he said.

'It did, in a way. This is about an experience one of the band members had. He asked a girl out, and she turned him down because she was, and I imagine still is, a lesbian,' Cecilia told Jude.

'Can you write a song about that? Don't it offend people?' Jude questioned.

Cecilia shrugged. 'This song *did* offend some people, but I'm not sure why. I imagine that people ask out people who aren't attracted to them all the time. A man asked out my best friend last week. She's not attracted to that man, or any man for that matter, so she politely rejected him. He told her she hadn't met the right man yet. That's offensive, but I don't personally think this song is. Then again, I'm not a lesbian. Even if I was, I couldn't speak for all lesbians,' she replied.

'That's stupid! If when I'd made it clear I were attracted to you, you'd said you was gay or whatever that one is where you're not attracted to anyone, I'd have been disappointed, but I wouldn't have questioned it. I wouldn't have said you wasn't what you are. Besides, there's more to attraction than gender. You didn't dump me cos I'm a man. You dumped me cos I'm an idiot. There ain't a label for not dating idiots,' Jude said.

Unbeknownst to Jude, this speech made Cecilia respect him a lot more. She might not be a lesbian or "whatever that one is where you're not attracted to anyone", but she *was* bisexual, which she'd been abused for in the past. The knowledge that Jude was open-minded about sexual orientation almost made her over-look the fact that in other ways, he was an idiot.

'If only more people thought like you, Jude,' Cecilia said.

While talking to Cecilia, Jude had felt calm, because he'd forgot-ten they were driving to his sister's student house to confirm that she was pregnant. A road sign informing drivers that they were 10 miles from Cambridge reminded him.

'What if she don't know who the father is?' Jude wondered out loud.

Even while talking to Jude, Cecilia hadn't forgotten why they were on the road, so she knew exactly what he was talking about. 'Does it matter if she doesn't know who the father is? We don't even know that she is pregnant yet. If she is, all that matters is how she feels about it, and what she intends to do about it. You are aware, by the way, that it'd be her choice what to do if she is pregnant, and she should feel supported in whatever she chooses,' she replied.

'She won't have an abortion, if that's what you're thinking. She's one of them who thinks it's murder,' Jude said. His head then fell into his hands. 'She's only nineteen, and now her life might be over!' Jude cried.

There were many things Cecilia could say to that. She believed abortion was a woman's choice and that a foetus had no life until birth, so it wasn't murder. As she'd just been talking about it being Millie's choice, it felt unnecessary and inappropriate to voice her opinions.

'There are other options besides abortion. *If* your sister is preg-nant, and *if* she wanted to, she could give birth and then give the baby up for adoption. Having a baby doesn't mean your life's over though. You can work while still being a parent. I could still do my job if I had children, as long as they were school-age,' Cecilia said, deciding to mention facts rather than opinions.

'You think so? Is Millie gonna be alright?' Jude questioned.

'Definitely. The important thing is that you support her. If *you* act like this is the end of the world, *she'll* think it's the end of the world. You must be positive, and you must let her make whatever choices she chooses to make,' Cecilia replied.

Jude took a deep breath. 'Thank God for you. I'd be useless without you,' he said.

Cecilia scoffed. 'Jude, this isn't about you, or me. It's about Millie. The fact that she called you, not another family member or a friend, says she thinks you can help. If you keep her in mind, you, and she, will be fine,' she told Jude.

'I guess we'll find out if I can help her soon,' Jude said.

*

CHAPTER TWENTY

When Jude knocked on Millie's door, it was opened almost instantly.

'I heard the car. I'm so glad you're here, Jude,' Millie said.

After greeting her brother, Millie gazed quizzically at Cecilia.

For a moment, Cecilia was distracted by how similar yet different Millie's eyes were to her brother's. They were the same colour and shape, but didn't have the twinkle Jude's had. When Millie blinked, Cecilia refocused and understood the question the eyes that had momentarily mesmerised her were asking.

'I drove Jude here. Don't worry, I'll make myself scarce,' Cecilia told Millie.

'Oh, alright then. I wouldn't have minded you staying, you know. I might not know who you are, but I'd have liked to have a woman around. Besides, you might one day be my sister-in-law. I ought to get to know you,' Millie replied.

'Sorry Millie, but she won't be your sister-in-law. We ain't a couple,' Jude hastily told his sister.

Millie frowned. 'Oh. That's a shame,' she said.

Feeling that she'd made things awkward, Millie walked into the house she shared with four other Cambridge University students.

Feeling that she ought to, Cecilia followed Millie into her house. Jude followed suit for the same reason.

'My best friend is a student. Your house smells a lot nicer than hers. Then again, she and her housemates are *medical* students, so perhaps that's why,' Cecilia commented when she saw the lounge, which the front door opened into.

The comment made Millie smile.

'We drew up a thorough cleaning rota which we stick to religiously. We didn't want our place to be like other student digs,' Millie revealed. Her tone belied how house-proud she was.

As she walked through the house, Millie gestured at sparkling surfaces, crumbless carpets, and dust-free knick-knacks. Cecilia made noises that indicated she was suitably impressed.

'No-one home?' Jude questioned when they reached the bright and empty kitchen at the back of the house.

'No. They've all got lectures, or research to do at the library. I do too, but I can't face it. I can't think about thinking, or anything but being pregnant,' Millie replied with a frown.

Ever since she'd walked into the house, Cecilia had been looking for an opportunity to mention the thing they were there for. This was the perfect opportunity. 'You might feel better once you've taken a test,' she suggested.

'Totally! Then you'll know what's what. Whatever it says, I love you little sis, and I'll help you with whatever you decide to do if you are pregnant,' Jude added.

A lone tear fell from Millie's left eye when she blinked. She did not speak.

'Do you have a test already? I carry a couple in my bag, and I can go to the shop if there's a specific one you want,' Cecilia said.

'I'm such a wuss that I couldn't pick one up and buy it,' Millie replied.

'You're not a wuss, little sis. This is a big thing. Not a good thing or a bad thing, you understand, but totally a big thing,' Jude told Millie.

On Cecilia's shoulder was her white leather bag. She rummaged around in it for almost a minute before producing a pregnancy test, still in its box, which she handed over to Millie.

'I'll erm… I'll just be a minute,' Millie said.

Under the watchful gaze of Jude and Cecilia, Millie shuffled out of the room on her way to the privacy of the bathroom upstairs.

-

For the first minute or so of Millie's absence, Jude and Cecilia stood in silence. The silence was broken when Jude said: 'I'm impressed that you had pregnancy tests in your bag.'

As if she was proud of it, Cecilia patted her bag. 'I've got all sorts in here. Pregnancy tests, a condom, a tampon, a crepe bandage, plasters, painkillers, cigarettes, cigarette lighter, and goodness knows what else,' she told Jude.

'Blimey! What on Earth are you preparing yourself for? Do I even wanna know?' Jude asked.

Cecilia guffawed. 'I don't intend to use all these items in one go, and I don't want to imagine an event that would require me to. They're not for *me*, anyway. I carry these things in case other people need them,' she replied.

'So you have a bag full of stuff for other people? That's nice,' Jude said.

'My purse and phone are in here. They're not for other people. I'm not that nice,' Cecilia pointed out.

Jude chuckled at this.

-

After the conversation about Cecilia's bag was complete, silence fell again.

The kitchen remained silent until Millie called down: 'It's been long enough now!'

'Do we go upstairs then?' Jude asked Cecilia.

'Yes. That's exactly what we do. This is what we came here for,' Cecilia replied.

Hand in hand, Jude and Cecilia walked up the beige-carpeted staircase. Upon reaching the landing, they found the bathroom door already open, so they entered the room.

'Will you look at it, Jude?' Millie asked.

'Yeah, if you want me to,' Jude replied.

The few steps to the side of the bath where Millie had left the test felt like a marathon to Jude.

'Never thought I'd hold something that my sister has peed on,' Jude commented as he picked up the test.

'What does it say?' Millie asked.

'There's one line. That means negative, don't it?' he replied.

As if she was the expert in pregnancy tests, Millie looked to Cecilia to answer. Just in case Jude had read it wrong, Cecilia took the test from him to examine herself.

'Yes, it's negative,' Cecilia confirmed.

Millie squealed. 'That's great! I'm so relieved!' she cried.

Cecilia decided not to mention that sometimes, tests were wrong.

'If I'm not pregnant, why haven't I had my period?' Millie questioned.

'Why don't we go downstairs and talk about it? I'd like to sit down,' Cecilia suggested.

Full of energy thanks to her negative result, Millie rushed down the stairs. This suited Cecilia, because she wanted to ask Jude a couple of questions out of earshot of his sister.

'Has her weight changed much?' Cecilia asked.

'Nah, she's always been a bit cuddly,' Jude replied.

'Is she stressed?' Cecilia questioned.

'I dunno. Today is the first time she's called me in nearly a year,' Jude answered.

Having asked Jude questions she didn't want Millie to hear, Cecilia now wanted to ask *Millie* questions she didn't want *Jude* to hear.

'Why don't you make us some tea, Jude?' Cecilia suggested.

As he couldn't see a reason not to make tea, Jude did as he was told. This left Cecilia alone in the lounge with Millie.

'University is hard, isn't it?' Cecilia said.

'Well, yeah. That's why you have to do all the exams to get in, and dedicate yourself to yet more exams once you're in. Uni life can be a riot though,' Millie replied.

That response was too flippant for Cecilia's liking. She'd have to be persistent to get an answer she was satisfied with.

'You strike me as the kind of girl who's motto is: "Work hard; play hard". Am I right?' Cecilia asked.

'Totally! What's the point of being here otherwise. If I don't work hard, I can't keep up, and if I'm gonna work hard, then I may as well play hard,' Millie replied.

'That attitude is what's lead to this,' Cecilia said. This was a bold thing to say, but she felt bold. She'd felt bold ever since Jude had told her about Millie's predicament.

That one sentence stunned Millie so much that all she could say in response was: 'What?'

'Your "work hard" attitude has made you stressed, which I think is why your period is late. I'm guessing that your "play hard" attitude has lead to unprotected sex, which is why when you were late, you assumed you were pregnant,' Cecilia explained.

What Cecilia said was true; Millie knew this. In that moment, sitting on her worn grey fabric sofa, she questioned every decision she'd made since leaving home. She hadn't questioned those decisions when she'd made them, but she was questioning them now.

'You alright, little sis?' Jude asked as he strolled into the room with two mugs of tea.

'Yeah. I am now,' Millie replied.

'Ain't it a miracle what a difference peeing on a stick can make?' Jude said.

Little did Jude know just how much of a difference his visit had made, not because of the pregnancy test, but because of Cecilia. To Millie, that woman was a miracle.

*

CHAPTER
TWENTY-ONE

Trumptington Street was packed full of pedestrians, disturbingly-fast-moving cyclists, and motor vehicles. Jude and Cecilia knew this, for they were among the pedestrians. Cecilia didn't feel up to driving immediately, so on her request, she and Jude were wandering around Cambridge city centre. As Trumptington Street was one of the streets in that city centre, they'd ended up on it, as had dozens of other people.

'What's that?' Jude asked, pointing at a golden circle behind some glass on the corner of a building.

'It's the Corpus Clock,' Cecilia told Jude.

'That's a clock? A clock that tells time?' Jude questioned.

'Yes,' Cecilia confirmed.

The Corpus Clock had attracted a crowd of people. A crowd so big, it was identifiable as a crowd separate from the mass of people making their way around the city with no interest in one of its most famous monuments. Jude joined that crowd to take a closer look at the Clock. It was a rippled golden circle, almost bigger than him, with no numbers or hands.

'What's the point of it? What makes it any better than a normal clock?' Jude questioned.

Somewhere behind Jude, a man laughed at his comment. The man stopped laughing when Cecilia glared at him.

'The hordes of tourists admiring it makes it better than normal clocks,' Cecilia told Jude.

The hordes of tourists admiring the clock at that present moment, most of whom had heard Cecilia's comment, made sure not to meet her eye.

'Shall we move on?' Cecilia suggested.

'Yup,' agreed Jude, who was blushing slightly.

There was a little side road off of Trumptington Street that Cecilia lead Jude down. It was much quieter than Trumptington Street, despite having a quaint little church beside it that Jude considered to be far more attractive than the bizarre Corpus Clock.

On the opposite side of the road to the church was a pub, which had a blue plaque on the side.

'What's special about that pub?' Jude asked.

'If I'm right, Francis Crick strolled in there one day and announced: "I've found the secret of life!", or something like that. What the plaque fails to mention is Rosalind Franklin's involvement in DNA research,' Cecilia told Jude.

Jude scoffed. 'Ain't that just typical? Not walking into a pub and claiming you've discovered the secret of life, though in some places that might be typical. I mean men taking credit for a woman's work is typical,' he replied.

'It definitely is,' Cecilia agreed.

–

The quiet road lead to a market, which was busier; because it was busy, Jude and Cecilia walked straight past it. As they did so, a large and pompous building came into view.

'That's huge, and so grand!' Jude cried when he saw the large and pompous building.

'It's one of the colleges,' Cecilia told him.

Jude frowned at this knowledge, and Cecilia noticed his shoulders slump.

'Are you okay?' Cecilia asked Jude.

Jude sighed. 'Yeah, I'm fine. I don't know if it's cos I'm not the brightest or what, but I feel so unimportant and just not good enough in this city. There's knowledge everywhere, except in my head. It's like every building is judging me or something,' he told Cecilia. Jude then shook his head. 'Sorry, that probably sounds stupid to you. It's just cos I'm an idiot,' he said.

'I can tell you that it's *not* because you're an idiot. Tamsyn, a woman I couldn't love more who got A star across the board in her A-levels, has similar feelings about Cambridge. Her university have a campus here that she could have studied her course at, but when she came for an open day, she felt inferior to everyone and everything around her. Apparently she felt so bad here that she considered staying in Cornwall, which really says something. Thankfully, she found out that Chelmsford offer the same course, and she feels comfortable there,' Cecilia replied.

Knowing that it wasn't just him who felt the way he did about Cambridge comforted Jude. He no longer felt like an idiot.

'What's your thoughts on the place? You know loads about it. Have you been before?' Jude asked Cecilia.

'I *love* Cambridge! There's history at every turn, and I think that's most *brilliant*! I find the idea that this has all been the same for hundreds of years thrilling. If I'd have wanted to go to university, I'd have studied here, if they'd have let me. Mum *did* study here, and she told me lots of bits of trivia about the city. As it was, the career I wanted, freelance proofreading, doesn't require a degree. Colchester has a great deal of history, and I don't have to put myself in debt to live there, so that worked out okay,' Cecilia enthused.

As he hadn't bothered to ask about it (though he had made assumptions on their first date), this was the first time Jude had learned anything about Cecilia's work and education. Now he knew a little bit, he wanted to know more.

'So you could have gone to uni, you just didn't want to?' Jude questioned.

'I didn't *need* to. I'm not as bright as Tamsyn, but I had good enough grades to apply to most universities; it just would have been pointless. I knew I had a natural aptitude for spotting errors, I love books, and the world of publishing fascinates me, so proofreading was the natural career choice, and I didn't need to get myself into thousands of pounds worth of debt to do that,' Cecilia explained.

'Sounds like you're passionate about it, and that's what matters,' Jude said.

Cecilia beamed. 'I am. I love what I do. It's perfect for me,' she replied.

'By the sounds of it, *you're* perfect for *it*,' Jude told Cecilia.

'Perfect is stretching it, but I'm definitely good at it,' Cecilia replied.

From somewhere behind Jude and Cecilia, the clock bells of Great St Mary's chimed to tell all those in earshot that it was five o'clock.

'Odd. I thought I just heard Big Ben, but that's in London,' Jude said.

'Oh, I did too. The chime of Big Ben was based on a church clock near here,' Cecilia replied.

As well as confusing Jude, the chiming church clock bells prompted Cecilia to sigh and say: 'I think we should head back now.'

*

CHAPTER TWENTY-TWO

The modest mid-terrace Jude shared with Floyd lacked off-street parking, but as many residents of the street it was on lacked cars, Cecilia was able to park her Mini right outside the house.

'I can't thank you enough for today. What you did meant the world to me, *and* Millie. You was so awesome! I dunno how you did it!' Jude enthused a few seconds after Cecilia had put her handbrake on.

'I'm glad to have helped,' Cecilia replied.

'I think I'm *more* glad! You was totally awesome! I totally lost my cool, but you were all level-headed and clever. I dunno how you did it,' Jude said.

Usually, when someone complimented Cecilia, she questioned the sincerity of the speaker. That wasn't the case with Jude, for she didn't believe him capable of lying that convincingly.

There was something about the tight confines of a Mini Cooper, and being complimented so wholeheartedly, that made Cecilia want to be open. That was just as well, because to answer Jude truthfully, she'd have to reveal something that only one other person in the world knew about her.

'I called on Lia,' Cecilia told Jude.

'Leah? Who's Leah?' Jude questioned.

'Not *Leah*, *Lia*, as in the nickname for Cecilia. She's a capable, mischievous, and downright dominant version of me. A sort of alter-ego,' Cecilia explained.

In the few seconds it took Jude to form a response, Cecilia felt nauseous. She convinced herself that he'd think she was weird.

'That's so cool. I gotta say, I like Lia. I'm honoured to have met her. She's awesome!' Jude replied. Then Jude groaned inwardly as he realised his message might come across wrong. 'Not that normal Cecilia ain't awesome. She *is* awesome, and I like her. Of course, Lia ain't not normal, not in a bad way anyway,' he added. Feeling he still wasn't getting his message across correctly, Jude groaned outwardly. 'What I'm trying to say is that I like both everyday Cecilia and Lia, and they're both awesome,' Jude concluded.

The obvious awkwardness Jude felt made Cecilia titter. 'I understood, and I'm glad you like Lia. I *love* her. It was her that kissed you in the burger restaurant. I could never kiss like that as myself, but I can as Lia. I'd be her every day if I could, but I can't always call her up on demand. I'm lucky she made an appearance today. Most often, she evades me. When I was waiting for you in The Tower's Shadow, I spent some of my time trying to become her. I thought if I could be Lia in a setting as intimate as a dinner date, it might lead to things. Obviously, it didn't. I stayed as plain old Cecilia, and by the time you turned up, I'd lost all interest in "things",' she replied.

Ever since they'd left Millie's house, Jude had been looking for an opportunity to talk to Cecilia about that fateful date. He knew he wasn't going to get a better opportunity than this one.

'I'm sorry about what I did that day, and I'm even more sorry for not understanding how much it hurt you. I just didn't get it, but I do now,' Jude said.

'You "get it", do you? How come? What's changed?' Cecilia questioned. She wasn't prepared to take Jude's apology at face value. Lia's influence hadn't completely faded yet.

'I talked to Floyd about it. I'd thought you was just bored or something. I didn't know that actually, you spent an hour or more beating yourself up, trying to find a fault that weren't there. I'm lucky enough to have never felt that way, so it never occurred to me that anyone would. It were only when Floyd told me how you felt that night that I realised what I'd done. He knew we'd kissed on the date before, so he thought you might have thought you'd scared me off. I'm totally sorry, Cecilia. You didn't scare me off at all. I loved that kiss, and I love you,' Jude revealed.

Not for a second did Cecilia doubt the sincerity of Jude's apology. The raw emotional atmosphere it created in her small car made her want to crumble and cry. Her first instinct was to accept Jude's apology unreservedly, and offer to get back together with him. She bit her tongue to prevent herself doing that. He'd hurt her badly, and it would take more than an apology to prove he deserved to be her partner. Ignoring her instincts, Cecilia thought up an alternative plan.

'That's exactly how I felt. Floyd is very wise, and so are you for listening to him. I accept your apology, because I can see that you mean it,' Cecilia said.

Jude smiled. 'Thanks. You didn't have to do that, and it means a lot to me,' he told Cecilia.

Moving onto the second part of her plan, Cecilia asked: 'I don't feel like dating again, but would you be interested in being friends?'

The smile on Jude's face widened. 'Totally! I'd like that a lot. You're generous to offer that,' he replied.

'I like you, Jude. You'd be a great friend for me,' Cecilia said.

Sitting in Cecilia's Mini, outside the house he'd go into in a minute once he'd said grateful goodbyes, Jude decided he'd do everything in his power to be "a great friend".

*

CHAPTER TWENTY-THREE

The business cards Jude had had made by a local printers, and the website he'd set up with help from a friend of Morton's, both bore his landline phone number as well as his mobile. This meant that clients often left messages for him on the answerphone.

Often, when Jude got home from being out somewhere, he'd check the answerphone while waiting for the kettle to boil. If Floyd had been home while he hadn't, Jude would sometimes ask him if he had any messages for him, and if he wanted tea. Occasionally, Floyd *volunteered* information and hot drinks requests.

'Jude, there's a message on the machine that I think is for you. Either that or they got the wrong number. It certainly isn't for me,' Floyd said to Jude one day.

'Oh really? What was it?' Jude questioned. The strange way Floyd had informed him about the message suggested it wasn't just a simple business request.

'Erm, I can't really describe it. Why don't you just play it?' Floyd replied.

This piqued Jude's curiosity. Hoping for a new client, he made his way to the answerphone machine, which was on a windowsill at the bottom of the stairs, and pressed play.

'Message seven. Received today at eleven twelve am,' a crisp pre-recorded female voice told Jude through the speaker of the answerphone machine.

'I'm having a period!' a much less crisp pre-recorded female voice cried through the speaker of the same answerphone machine.

The sound of his little sister's voice made Jude smile. It was better than any work he could wish for. The idea of Floyd listening to that message and wondering who would leave that message and why also made Jude smile. Floyd would never know, for although Jude told him everything about himself, he'd kept Millie's situation to himself. Only he and Cecilia knew about it.

'Message six. Received yesterday at five oh five pm,' the answerphone's crisp voice said.

Even though he knew what message six said, Jude let it play.

'Hello, Jude! I'm calling from home, hence why I've called *you* at home. I hope that's okay. I know most people only use mobiles these days, but I'm behind the times. I just wanted to let you know my birthday picnic will be at two on Sunday, not one. I've convinced Tamsyn to come, and as I'm going to pick her up, I'll be a bit late. Sorry for changing plans. Please let me know if this doesn't work for you. Tamsyn has offered to drive herself to Colchester, but I'd like to save her the petrol if I can. I hope this is all okay. Don't hesitate to call me if it isn't,' Cecilia's voice told Jude, just as it already had four times before.

'Why wouldn't it be okay? I ain't got work that weekend, just like most weekends, and some weeks,' Jude replied, even though he knew the answerphone machine couldn't hear him. As the name suggests, it was made to answer the phone, not Jude. Otherwise it would be called the answerJude machine.

Before the machine could play message five, Jude stopped it. He then strolled into the lounge, where Floyd was lounging on the green corduroy sofa.

'Was that message for you?' Floyd asked.

'Yeah. Thanks for telling me about it,' Jude replied.

'No problem. Did you listen to Cecilia again while you were there?' Floyd asked.

'Of course. I can't help it. The way she speaks is great. I mean, it kind of reminds me of Constance, which ain't great, but proper English sounds so much better coming from Cecilia than it ever did from her,' Jude told Floyd.

At the mention of Constance, Floyd grimaced. 'Trust me, Jude, Cecilia isn't Constance,' he said.

Jude nodded. 'Nah. She totally ain't,' he agreed.

*

CHAPTER TWENTY-FOUR

Pretty parks are rarely peaceful, for their prettiness attracts people. This was the case with Colchester's Castle Park. It did have quiet moments, but the Sunday Cecilia had chosen to celebrate her birthday in the park wasn't one of them. Jude discovered this when he stumbled upon the spot where the birthday-girl-to-be was sitting on a picnic blanket with Tamsyn and Emma-Leigh.

When she saw Jude, Emma-Leigh looked him up and down and winced. 'Your jeans are covered in paint! They've got rips in too! *Unfashionable* rips!' she cried.

Jude looked down at his jeans, which had a few dried splatters of white emulsion on them. 'Yup. Good enough for the park though, ain't they?' he replied.

'No! They should never see the light of day!' Emma-Leigh argued.

'That's funny. I thought I were wearing jeans, not vampires,' Jude said.

As Jude intended, his comment made Cecilia titter. It also made Tamsyn cackle.

Apart from laughing, there was no way to respond to Jude's witty remark; at least, no way that Emma-Leigh could think of. She got to her feet, but did not speak.

'Do you find my jeans so offensive that you can't bare to look at them?' Jude questioned.

Once again, Cecilia tittered, though Tamsyn remained silent this time.

'I'm just going to nip to the little girl's room. I can see you brought cake, so I think I'll put up with your truly awful clothes,' Emma-Leigh replied.

While Emma-Leigh strolled off in the direction of the public toilets, Jude got comfortable on the picnic blanket. He handed the white carrier bag full of goodies from The Lion Walk Bakery over to Cecilia.

'Happy birthday,' Jude said.

'Ooh, is it all for me then?' Cecilia asked.

'Only if you never want to see me again,' Tamsyn replied.

The bag had four polystyrene boxes in it, each containing a slice of red velvet cake. While frowning, Cecilia slid a box over to Tamsyn.

Jude wasn't the only one who'd brought something to the picnic. From her jeans pocket, Tamsyn produced birthday cake candles, which she handed to Cecilia, saying: 'Happy birthday.'

'Thank you, Tamsyn. Thank you too, Jude,' Cecilia said.

'It's cool,' Jude replied.

'It's the least I can do,' Tamsyn told Cecilia.

Not wanting Emma-Leigh to miss out, Cecilia left the sweet-smelling cake untouched. Tamsyn and Jude followed her lead.

Having distributed the cake and candles, Jude, Cecilia, and Tamsyn, had nothing to say to each other. This doesn't mean they sat in silence. The tweeting of birds and chatter of the many picnicking park-goers created constant noise, just not conversation between the three.

As she had arranged the picnic, Cecilia felt uncomfortable about the lack of conversation. She felt like she'd failed at being a host.

When she thought of a question to ask Jude, she felt an extreme sense of relief.

'How is your sister, Jude?' Cecilia asked.

'Great, thanks to you. Emily left a message to say she is having a period, so that's all good now,' Jude replied.

'I certainly did *not*, and it's *Emma-Leigh*, not *Emily*,' said Emma-Leigh, from behind Jude.

Because he had his back to the loos, Jude hadn't seen Emma-Leigh approaching, so her voice made him jump, which made Cecilia titter, Tamsyn cackle, and Emma-Leigh chortle.

'I were talking about my sister. Her name is Emily, but I normally call her Millie,' Jude told Emma-Leigh.

Now that Emma-Leigh was back, Cecilia handed her a box with cake in, and candles. She fished a cigarette lighter out of her white leather shoulder bag, which she used to light the candles that were stuck in the cake slices.

Jude, Tamsyn, and Emma-Leigh glanced at each other and grinned. They knew they all had the same thought.

'Shall I start us off?' Emma-Leigh asked.

'Start what?' Cecilia questioned.

'One, two, three...' Emma-Leigh said.

Instead of continuing her countdown, Emma-Leigh started singing *Happy Birthday*, and Jude and Tamsyn joined in.

When the song ended, Cecilia blew out the candle on her slice of cake. In turn, Jude, Tamsyn, and Emma-Leigh presented their candles for blowing out.

'You do know I'm *twenty*-four, not *four*?' Cecilia questioned.

'You're never too old for a singsong. Now, eat your cake, birthday girl,' Emma-Leigh insisted.

'My actual birthday is next week,' Cecilia pointed out.

'Are you saying you don't want to eat cake? I certainly do,' Emma-Leigh questioned.

In answer to Emma-Leigh's question, Cecilia nibbled her cake, and continued to do so for the next five minutes.

-

Eating cake causes a cessation of conversation, but that's okay because eating good cake is an all-consuming and immensely enjoyable experience.

When conversation resumes after consuming cake, it is usually about the quality of the cake. This was the case at Cecilia's birthday picnic.

Cecilia proclaimed the cake was: 'Exquisite!'

Tamsyn declared the cake to be: 'Yummy.'

Emma-Leigh told everyone in earshot the cake was: 'Delicious!'

Jude said the cake was: 'Alright.'

With no food to distract them, Cecilia and her friends discreetly turned their attention to a couple who were walking past slowly, as if they'd never seen a town park and didn't want to miss a single tree or daisy. The couple consisted of a woman in Ray-Ban's, straw boater, and a lightweight white dress with flowers embroidered into it; and a man in neon yellow top and neon green shorts.

'Wow! Have you seen the castle?' neon-clad man asked his partner.

'Yes dear. I don't know how I could *not* see it,' cliché-summer-attire-wearing woman replied.

'But there's actually a castle! It's the town centre and there's a castle!' neon-clad man cried.

Something about this comment made cliché-summer-attire-wearing woman stop and stare at her partner. 'Darling, what is this park called?' she asked.

There was a momentary pause while neon-clad man checked in his head that he actually knew the answer to the question. 'Well, it's Castle Park, but I didn't think it would genuinely have a castle in it. There's not an admiral in Admiral's Park,' he replied.

Cliché-summer-attire-wearing woman laughed at her partner. 'Bless you, darling. You're not the brightest, are you?' she said.

Neon-clad man shook his head. 'I guess not,' he admitted.

'And to think I have a PhD. Sometimes, I wonder why we're married,' cliché-summer-attire-wearing woman told her partner.

'I thought it was because we loved each other. Don't we love each other?' neon-clad man questioned.

Cliché-summer-attire-wearing woman laughed so hard that she had to hold her straw boater to stop it falling off her head. 'Of course we love each other, you silly sod. I was teasing. Can't you take a joke?' she replied.

Neon-clad man blushed so hard that his cheeks were almost as brightly-coloured as his clothes. 'I guess not,' he said.

The neon-clad man had curly blonde hair, which cliché-summer-attire-wearing woman ruffled. 'I'd have thought you'd have learnt after ten years. I'm not being malicious,' she told him.

Cecilia and her friends never got to hear the man's response, for the couple moved out of their hearing range. The four of them exchanged a look that conveyed their distaste to each other.

'That poor man being with that woman. He shouldn't put up with being treated like that,' Tamsyn commented.

Emma-Leigh's nostrils flared, and she emited a short, sharp, shriek. 'What would you know about what it takes to make a relationship work these days?' she asked.

The sharp tone Emma-Leigh used made Tamsyn sit up straight,

as did the way she interpreted her words. 'You can't say that! What makes you a relationship expert? How many times has your partner cheated on you now?' Tamsyn snapped.

'Twice, but I give him more attention now, and he's promised to never do it again,' Emma-Leigh replied. In one sentence, her voice went from being as harsh as sandpaper, to as soft as the grass around the picnic blanket she was sitting on.

A few seconds later, Emma-Leigh found there were hot tears rolling down her cheeks. Upon discovering this, she started sobbing, and those hot tears became part of a stream.

Cecilia glared at Tamsyn. 'That was so out of order!' she growled at her.

'*She* was!' Tamsyn replied.

Instead of using her mouth to answer Tamsyn, Cecilia used her eyebrows.

'I can't believe you can't see it!' Tamsyn cried.

Without waiting for an answer, Tamsyn stormed off, leaving a sobbing Emma-Leigh, a raging Cecilia, and a dumbfounded Jude, sitting on a picnic blanket gazing uncomfortably at their laps.

'Should I follow her?' Jude asked.

'Yes. See what she has to say for herself,' Cecilia replied.

-

By the time Jude had caught up with Tamsyn, she'd made it to an orderly garden, which was situated in the shadow of a grand Georgian house and surrounded a water feature. The tranquil setting seemed at odds with Tamsyn's mood.

'What's got you so hot and bothered?' Jude asked Tamsyn.

'It's discrimination! She wouldn't have said that to a straight person!' Tamsyn snapped back.

'Sorry. I didn't know you ain't straight,' Jude said, because he was sorry, and he hadn't known Tamsyn wasn't straight. He felt like he'd missed something, and made a prat of himself as a result.

Suddenly, something dawned on Tamsyn. '*She* didn't know either! Emma-Leigh *can't* have been discriminating; she didn't know there was anything to discriminate against!' she cried.

'What?' Jude questioned.

'I've made a stupid mistake, and I need to make amends,' Tamsyn told him, rushing out of the garden to do just that.

Unsure of what mistake Tamsyn had made or what to do, Jude followed her.

*

CHAPTER
TWENTY-FIVE

Pretty parks are rarely peaceful, for their prettiness attracts people, and when those people are hurt and insulted, some of them sob. This was the case when Emma-Leigh Layton visited Castle Park to celebrate Cecilia's birthday and was insulted by Tamsyn.

'Oh, I've really upset you, haven't I? I shouldn't have said what I said. I'm so sorry,' Tamsyn said to Emma-Leigh when she returned from the garden she'd stormed off to.

'No, of course you shouldn't have said what you said! What were you thinking, Tamsyn?!' Emma-Leigh snapped.

'I was thinking that you were picking on me for my orientation. I've had more than enough of that in my life, which is why I bit back so ferociously. I now know though, that you weren't doing that at all. How could you? You don't know my orientation,' Tamsyn told Emma-Leigh.

Cecilia, who had been cradling Emma-Leigh while she cried, looked questioningly at Jude, who had followed Tamsyn. Jude shrugged as if to say: "I don't know".

Thanks to Cecilia's comforting embrace, Emma-Leigh's tears had dried up.

'No, I don't know your orientation. Do you think it would make a difference if I did?' Emma-Leigh questioned.

'In my experience, yes. The moment anyone finds out I'm asexual, they start treating me differently, with the notable exception of Cecilia and one guy in school,' Tamsyn replied.

A conversation Jude had had with Cecilia in her Mini came back to him. 'Oh, yeah! That's that one where you're not attracted to anyone! That's what it is, ain't it?!' he cried.

'Erm, yes. An asexual person is a person who doesn't experience sexual attraction. That's what *I* mean when I call myself asexual. I'm not romantically or sexually attracted to anyone,' Tamsyn explained.

'Why would I care about that?' Emma-Leigh questioned.

So many times, Tamsyn had wondered why *anyone* would care about her orientation. It was *her* orientation. Why should anyone care about it? Unfortunately for her, many people, her own parents and most of their neighbours included, *did* care about it, and they made their feelings known. This was why Tamsyn was so surprised by Jude and Emma-Leigh's reactions.

'Aren't you going to question me or tell me I'm wrong?' Tamsyn asked.

'Nah, it's your sexuality. I'm happy to accept you're right about it. If you ain't, what does it matter to me? I had no plans to hit on you, or anyone actually, so I don't see what difference it makes to me,' Jude replied.

'I'm really not interested,' Emma-Leigh told Tamsyn.

Having revealed one of her few secrets and received a neutral reaction to it, Tamsyn sat still in stunned silence. She wasn't truly present at the picnic anymore. She was in Redruth and Chelmsford, listening to people tell her she couldn't be what she was. That she was mistaken about who she was. In her head, she laughed at those people and told them how ignorant they were. Tamsyn hadn't done that in real life. In real life, she had run to her bedroom, or the beach, or Cecilia's house, wherever she could be herself, and cried, and told herself how messed up she was in the head. Right now though, in Colchester, Tamsyn didn't feel the need to run. She didn't feel messed up in the head. She felt accepted. She felt safe.

Unheard by Tamsyn, Emma-Leigh said: 'You seem very quiet, Cecilia. Do you have a problem with what Tamsyn's just told us?'

'No, not at all. I already knew, so I feel no need to react. I've known for as long as I've known Tamsyn. She told me when we met,' Cecilia replied.

'Wow, that's openness and then some! Where did you meet, some kind of safe space?' Jude asked.

Thinking back to when she'd met Tamsyn made Cecilia cringe and smile at the same time. 'No, a cafe. I told Tamsyn that she was beautiful and I was attracted to her. She very politely turned me down, and I bought her cream tea to apologise for bothering her. We ended up sharing the cream tea, and while the tea was still hot, she told me *why* she'd turned me down. Thanks to her openness, as you put it, we've been friends ever since,' she told Jude.

'Cecilia made it a safe space. She's a real lifesaver. Her kindness was extraordinary,' Tamsyn commented.

'Well, she is kind, ain't she? I knew that. That's just Cecilia,' Jude said.

Emma-Leigh raised her bottle of Coke Zero Vanilla in the air. 'A toast to the birthday-girl-to-be?' she suggested.

Jude and Tamsyn raised their own bottled beverages and tapped them against Emma-Leigh's. They then unscrewed the caps and took sips of their drinks.

'Don't have the same impact when you do it with plastic bottles, does it?' Jude questioned.

There was a murmur of agreement from Cecilia, Tamsyn, and Emma-Leigh.

'I'm sorry, Cecilia. I've hijacked your celebration by snapping at

Emma-Leigh and then talking about myself,' Tamsyn said.

Cecilia smiled and replied: 'Don't be sorry. You feeling comfortable to share, and you being accepted, are perhaps the best presents I could ask for. This is the best birthday I've had since my eighteenth.'

The birthday was so good that, for the first time in years, Cecilia didn't think about the fact that her brother would also be celebrating his birthday.

*

CHAPTER TWENTY-SIX

'I like that we're merging our friendship groups. It's no bad thing to have more friends,' Cecilia said to Jude, Morton, and Emma-Leigh, all of whom were with her at The Colneside Snooker Club.

'This whole arrangement works extremely well for me. Without things like this, I shall forever have only the one friend, Jude here,' Morton replied.

'Do you honestly think that?' Cecilia questioned.

Morton laughed a laugh that was devoid of humour. 'I *know* so. I make terrible company,' he replied.

'You don't. I wouldn't be your friend if you were actually as dull as people tell you you are. I ain't *that* nice,' Jude told Morton.

As Morton wasn't used to being complimented, except on how intelligent he was or how well he played snooker, he didn't know how to answer Jude.

As she was at the snooker club to play snooker, Emma-Leigh asked: 'How do we play this?'

While Cecilia placed brightly-coloured balls precisely on white crosses and Morton told Emma-Leigh the basic rules of snooker, Jude listened to a young couple at the table in the corner kiss. He didn't *want* to listen to the couple kiss, but it was unavoidable.

When Cecilia's phone played *Oh, Cecilia (Breaking My Heart)* at full volume, the noisily-kissing couple stopped kissing. When the song stopped playing abruptly, the couple started playing snooker, which Jude was very thankful for.

'I knew it would be from him.' Cecilia said when she got her phone out of the butterscotch leather crossbody bag she was wearing.

'Who is him?' Emma-Leigh asked.

Inside his head, Jude said: *I'm glad you asked, Emma-Leigh, because I wanted to know too.'*

'Conner. He text me yesterday about arranging a birthday party for Dad,' Cecilia replied.

Inside his head, Jude said: '*Oh, just her brother. That's okay then.'*

'You refused, didn't you? Please tell me you refused,' Emma-Leigh said out loud.

Cecilia gazed at the worn burgundy carpet on the snooker room floor. 'I *can't* refuse. Mum would've organised the best day imaginable. It's not Conner's fault that she's not here to do that, and Dad still deserves a good party. I *have* to help,' she replied.

'Cecilia, you *can't* help. You know what happens when you do things with Conner,' Emma-Leigh argued.

'I'll do better this time. I won't get all caught up in the details, so I won't be so slow,' Cecilia insisted.

'He'll still pick on you, Cecilia. It's what he does,' Emma-Leigh told her in as soft a tone as she was capable of.

Because she knew what Emma-Leigh said was true, Cecilia didn't answer her. She just focused on the last few balls that needed to be placed.

'The table is ready. I'm sorry it took me so long,' Cecilia announced when she'd finished placing the balls.

To save money, Jude, Cecilia, Morton, and Emma-Leigh were all sharing one table. They played in pairs, Emma-Leigh and Morton verses Jude and Cecilia. Cecilia had subtly arranged the pairings to ensure fairness.

Cecilia got the game underway by playing the break-off shot. She had played the shot many times in the past, so the result was close to what she'd intended.

'Sorry,' Cecilia said to Jude as she walked away from the table.

'Erm, why? It's cool,' Jude replied.

'No, it's not. That isn't quite what I meant to play,' Cecilia told Jude.

Jude nodded at the table. 'I don't think you've got anything to worry about,' he murmured.

Leaning over the table awkwardly, gripping the cue she'd picked at random very tightly, was Emma-Leigh.

'You are joking, aren't you?' Morton asked Emma-Leigh.

In response, Emma-Leigh hit the cue ball with the butt of her cue. To no-one's surprise except her own, this resulted in her playing a foul shot and giving away four points to her opponents.

'I see that you were *not* joking. Emma-Leigh, we need to have a chat,' Morton said.

While Morton and Emma-Leigh had a chat, Jude sent a red ball straight into a pocket with no visible effort.

As they were taking alternate shots, Cecilia followed Jude's red with an unsuccessful attempt to pot the black.

'I messed up again! I can't believe it!' Cecilia cried.

'Chillax, Cecilia. It's just a game,' Jude told her.

As he so often did when he stood over a snooker table, Morton achieved exactly what he intended to. In this case, he had intended to make the red four foot from the left middle pocket disappear.

With great reluctance, Morton stood aside to let Emma-Leigh take her turn. Holding her cue the correct way round, she got down on her shot.

'Why are you aiming to glance off the pink? The black is easier and worth one more point. A point I think we'll need, based on your performance,' Morton questioned.

'Pink is prettier. It's my favourite colour. I am a girl, after all,' Emma-Leigh replied.

Morton sighed. 'That's an unconventional approach to shot selection, but I'll put up with it for this frame just to see what happens. I would like you to actually pot it, though,' he said.

'I will,' Emma-Leigh insisted.

'Not aiming like that you won't,' Morton told Emma-Leigh.

Before Emma-Leigh could play her shot wrong, Morton marched round the table, snatching the little blue-topped cube chalk on his way. He placed it on the side of the table and pointed at it. 'Aim for this. That will put the pink in the bottom right and leave the cue ball on a choice of three reds,' Morton ordered.

While pouting, Emma-Leigh did as she was told, and the pink rattled in the jaws of the pocket and refused to drop off the table.

'Close. We'll get there,' Morton declared.

-

"Get there" Morton and Emma-Leigh *did*, just about. Emma-Leigh eventually got good enough to play without shot-by-shot instructions. With Morton, she beat Jude and Cecilia by seven points.

Although Cecilia's plan to keep things evenly-matched worked, she felt uneasy. This was because while she and her friends were playing their evenly-matched frame of snooker, most of the time the only noises were the clicks and clacks of the balls, and the squelches and slurps from the mouths of the couple at the end of the room. She had intended for there to be light chatter.

Because Cecilia had played the first shot in the first frame, either Morton or Emma-Leigh had to break off the second frame. Emma-Leigh chose herself to play the break-off shot before Morton could stop her.

'Now, remember to use the narrow end of the big wooden stick. You ain't trying to break the little white ball. You're meant to gently tap it,' Jude told Emma-Leigh.

Desperate to keep conversation flowing, Cecilia said the first thing that came into her head, which was: 'May I have a dozen Granny Smith's, please?'

'What?' Jude questioned.

'You talk like you've just come off the market in Chelmsford, and they sell apples at markets, so I was making a joke about how you speak,' Cecilia explained.

Emma-Leigh chortled.

Jude made no sound, but his glaring grey eyes said it all. 'What a cow! I don't have money like you, and my family don't have a fancy shield thing, but that don't mean I ain't good enough for you! You didn't have to pretend not to know me when you ran into your mates,' he raged.

'What do you mean? I don't understand?' Cecilia questioned.

'You talk like an ex-girlfriend of mine, so I were talking to you as if you was her, just because you speak like her!' Jude snapped back.

Only one word came to Cecilia's mind. 'Sorry,' she whispered to Jude.

Jude shook his head. 'Yeah, you should be. I thought you wasn't like that,' he said.

'Sorry,' Cecilia replied.

'Sorry don't cut it. I'm gonna walk outta here before one of us says something else stupid,' Jude told Cecilia.

Without another word, Jude stormed out of the room.

'What have I done?' Cecilia asked, head in hands.

'You have accidentally reminded my friend of a horrible woman, and suffered the full force of his temper as a result,' Morton told Cecilia.

Neither Cecilia nor Emma-Leigh knew what to say to this. This meant they could hear the couple who were kissing at the end of the room all too well.

'Shut up! I can hear you from here! It's disgusting!' Emma-Leigh barked at the noisily-kissing couple.

At once, the couple disentangled.

'I told you so,' the woman said to her partner.

'It doesn't count. You deliberately snog loudly when we're out and about,' the man of the once-noisily-kissing couple replied.

The exchange made no sense to Emma-Leigh, and she wasn't in a mood where she was willing to accept things not making sense. 'What are you two going on about, and why did you think it was okay to make us all feel sick?' she asked.

The woman of the once-noisily-kissing couple blushed. 'We had a bet, Stefan and me. We both love PDAs, public displays of affection, but I know that many people don't. Once, when Stefan full-on French kissed me in McDonald's, I bet him that one day, someone would have a go. He told me that it's not the British way to actually tell people to stop doing something. They might tut, but they won't come over and say something. You have just proven him wrong, and won me a tenner,' she explained.

'That's ridiculous! Who does that?!' Emma-Leigh cried.

The woman (who hadn't given her name) and Stefan looked at each other. 'Erm, we do,' Stefan replied.

While Emma-Leigh had been snapping at the couple she considered to be ridiculous, Cecilia had started weeping.

'I have a suggestion to make. I believe it would be best for everyone if we just went back to our respective houses. This evening is a lost cause,' Morton said.

'But Jude! I've upset him!' Cecilia protested through her tears.

'And there is nothing you can do about that tonight. He'll have gone home peeved. If you wish to, you can make amends another day, when he's calmed down,' Morton told Cecilia.

Knowing Morton to be right, Cecilia followed his advice. She got no sleep that night, but she believed that was what she deserved.

*

CHAPTER TWENTY-SEVEN

Having only had a few hours sleep thanks to doubts about ever being able to be a competent paramedic, Tamsyn stumbled down to the shared kitchen to make herself a strong instant coffee.

Already in the shared kitchen when Tamsyn entered it was Scott, who was pouring boiling water into his mug of instant pasta. 'Morning. I'm guessing by the fact that you're having pasta in a mug for breakfast that you slept as well as I did,' she said to him. Despite her tiredness, she put on a bright and cheery tone.

'How would I know? I don't know how you slept. *No-one* knows how you sleep, and that won't change while you insist you're acesexual, or whatever you called it,' Scott replied.

Before Tamsyn could tell Scott she labelled herself as *asexual* or *ace*, and acesexual isn't a label, at least not one she'd heard of, he walked out of the room.

-

The strong coffee woke Tamsyn up a little bit, but she still felt far too tired to process her textbooks. That was a problem; she had to process her textbooks to pass her exams.

When *Ride of the Valkyries* blared out from Tamsyn's phone, she was very pleased. She was even more pleased when she saw it was Cecilia calling.

'Cecilia! Why are you calling?' Tamsyn asked.

'I saw your Facebook post about a bad nights sleep. It made me wonder if you had something on your mind, so I've called you to ask if you want to talk,' Cecilia told Tamsyn.

As talking would give her an excuse not to stare at her textbooks, Tamsyn did want to talk. 'I'd really appreciate a little chat, but I have nothing new or interesting to tell you. I couldn't sleep because I was worrying about failing my course, and now I'm so tired that my books don't make any sense, so it's now more likely that I will indeed fail my course,' she said.

'You won't fail, Tamsyn. You're the brightest and kindest person I've ever met. Intelligence and kindness are all you need, and you have both in abundance,' Cecilia replied.

'You have those qualities too, but you're not a paramedic,' Tamsyn pointed out.

'I'm not sure about that,' Cecilia said.

'I am. You are definitely *not* a paramedic,' Tamsyn told Cecilia.

A quiet titter came down the line.

After the quiet titter came the sound of feet pacing up and down a hard-floored room.

'How are you, Cecilia?' Tamsyn asked.

'I'm a snob. I'm a cow and a snob,' Cecilia replied.

'You are? I don't think so. I've never thought you were either of those things,' Tamsyn said.

Cecilia sighed. 'Neither did I, until yesterday, but I am. Jude called me a cow, and he was right to, because I'm a snob,' she told Tamsyn.

The footsteps Tamsyn could hear became faster. In her mind's eye, she could see Cecilia walking up and down her kitchen, tightly clutching her mobile. It was clear to Tamsyn that Cecilia needed to talk even more than she did.

'What happened? What did you say that you believe was snobbish?' Tamsyn asked.

Over the next minute, Tamsyn listened to a conversation Cecilia had had with Jude repeated word for word. She also listened to background information so detailed, she could picture the scene in the snooker club. Much more relevantly, she could imagine Cecilia's state of mind that night.

'That wasn't a nice thing to say, but I know you well enough to know you never meant to hurt Jude, unlike this ex of his, whoever she is. You blurted it out because you felt you ought to say something, and that was what came to mind,' Tamsyn said.

'Of course I didn't mean to hurt him, but I did, and no wonder. I'm gutted. I was enjoying having him in my life. I had dreams that one day, far into the future, I might ask him to be in my life forever. That won't be happening now. He hates me, and I can't blame him,' Cecilia replied.

Even though Cecilia couldn't see her, Tamsyn shook her head, tossing her ginger curls from side to side. 'I doubt that he hates you, and if he *does*, that says more about him than it does you. If he means that much to you, you should tell him,' she told Cecilia.

'Do you think it's that simple? I just tell him how I feel?' Cecilia questioned.

'Not quite. I think it would help if you sit in your favourite armchair and tell me how you're feeling first, and I don't mean how you're feeling about Jude. Something is up with you. It's unlike you to be as thoughtless as you were last night,' Tamsyn clarified.

–

After the rumbling of an electric kettle boiling, the splishes and splashes of the boiled water being poured into a mug, and footsteps on a hard floor and then carpet, came a sigh of satisfaction from Cecilia as she sank into her armchair.

'Conner got in contact a couple of days ago about Dad's fiftieth, which is coming up at the end of the year. He wants me to help him arrange a party. Mum would've organised an unforgettable day for him. She was so good at that sort of thing. She was good at a lot of things. Conner said that as she isn't here, as her children, he and I ought to do it together. He pointed out that it wouldn't be fair for Dad to lose his wife and not celebrate his fiftieth birthday. It's a good point, so I have to help. It just keeps worrying me that I'm going to mess it up. I'm not my mum. I wish I was, but I'm not,' Cecilia blurted out as soon as she was sat down.

Before answering, Tamsyn took a deep breath. Grief was a tricky subject, one she knew very little about, and she knew she had to take care. 'Taking into account what she knew about the way Conner treats you, what do you think your mum would've wanted?' she asked.

'If only I knew! What I wouldn't give for a five minute chat with her; just five minutes. Part of me thinks she'd tell Conner where to stick it. She could be like that sometimes. That's wishful thinking though. The more grown-up part of me tells me she'd want me to get along with Conner for Dad's sake. Dad doesn't know the extent of the rift between Conner and I, and it'd kill him if he did,' Cecilia replied.

What Tamsyn wanted to say was: "Your mum loved you. She wouldn't want you to have to suffer working with Conner". As she wasn't in Cecilia's mum's mind, and had never even met the woman, it seemed like an inappropriate thing to say. It also seemed inappropriate to advise Cecilia to help Conner with their dad's party. In conclusion, Tamsyn decided that she shouldn't advise Cecilia to do anything.

'I'm guessing that as the party wouldn't be until the end of the year, you have time to consider whether or not to assist Conner. Am I right?' Tamsyn questioned.

'He's asking me now though,' Cecilia said.

'That doesn't mean you have to answer straightaway,' Tamsyn pointed out.

There was a pause in conversation while Cecilia considered this. 'I suppose not, but I ought to let him know as soon as possible,' she eventually replied.

'I agree. I'm just suggesting you redefine possible,' Tamsyn said.

On Cecilia's end of the line, a tinny but tuneful melody started playing.

'Oh, that's the house phone! I should answer it. Sorry. I don't mean to be rude cutting you off, but the call might be work related,' Cecilia told Tamsyn.

'It's fine, Cecilia. I understand. Thank you for checking up on me,' Tamsyn replied.

Without another word, Cecilia hung up.

Tamsyn made a mental note to keep a closer eye on her best friend in future. She then made digital notes about her textbooks, which were now making more sense to her tired brain.

*

CHAPTER TWENTY-EIGHT

'I knew you didn't mean it. It's funny you called me here to apologise, cos I wanna apologise to you. I totally overreacted, and it ain't nothing to do with you; it's cos of some girl I were with in the past,' Jude told Cecilia. He then took a sip of the Americano she'd bought him. 'If I get nice coffee every time you upset me, then please feel free to do it again. This beats supermarket's own instant hands down,' Jude commented.

'Trinity do the best coffee in town. I'm glad you like it. I hope it goes some way to making amends for what I said,' Cecilia replied.

Before answering, Jude took another sip of his coffee. 'Like I said, it ain't about you. Luckily for you, you ain't never met Constance. She were the typical stuck-up rich girl, but for a while I were stupid enough to love her. I should point out that she were the one to ask me out, and I were working in her house when she did. I thought she were pretty, not in your league, but good enough, but I'd have never even spoken to a girl like her had she not slipped me her number one day,' he said.

Being told by Jude that it wasn't her fault he'd got upset helped Cecilia breathe easier. Guilt and anxiety were replaced by curiosity and sympathy.

'What made you think Constance is, and may well still be, stuck-up?' Cecilia questioned.

'We used to talk about our futures all the time. She were always gonna be Oxbridge; the only question were what course and what college, and she were taking a "gap year" to work that out. I already knew I were gonna be a painter and decorator. She told me to "better myself", as if being a painter and decorator ain't good enough. At the time, I thought she were just being nice. That she were looking out for me, you know? Anyway, that ain't how I know she's stuck-up and a snob. We was out in town one day, I were taking her for her first proper cafe fry-up, and we came across some of her mates. As soon as she spotted them, she gave me a shove and a look that I knew meant something but I couldn't work out what something. Turns out she wanted me to bug... to get lost. I didn't get the message, so I stuck around. One of her friends asks who I am, and Constance suddenly pretends not to know me. She acts like I'm some stranger and she's disgusted to be in my vicinity. Her friends all crowd round her and tell me to leave her alone, so I do,' Jude ranted, using his fingers for quotation marks.

Cecilia gasped. 'That's awful!' she cried.

'Yup. You can imagine how I felt. I went to her stables later that day cos I knew I'd find her there. I asked her what it was all about and she told me she couldn't be seen by her mates with "my sort". At the time, I didn't question the "my sort" thing; I were still in some fairyland. I only questioned when she intended braving it and telling people about us. To that she said, and I quote: "Well, never. We're just a bit of fun. A discreet bit of fun that will last until I head off to Oxford or Cambridge". It were more than fun for me; I could see a future with her. When I told her I wanted us to stay together long-term, she accused me of being after her money. That, that right there, was when I knew she were a snob,' Jude told Cecilia.

'What a horrible woman! I'm so sorry I reminded you of her,' Cecilia replied.

'You couldn't have known. Don't feel too sorry for me anyway, cos she had something of a point. I had thought about how nice it would be if she shared some of her money with me. I loved the idea of being rich *almost* as much as I loved her,' Jude said.

As she didn't know how to answer that, Cecilia didn't speak.

When Jude noticed how dry his throat was, he realised he'd done a lot of talking; too much talking, in his opinion.

To deal with the effect his excessive talking had had on his throat, Jude downed the remainder of his coffee.

To deal with the effect his excessive talking might have had on Cecilia, Jude said: 'No need to apologise. As I'm sure you can now see, you ain't like Constance. *I* should apologise for going on and on about my ex. I feel bad about that now.'

'Don't feel bad. We all do it. I could go on and on about my ex,' Cecilia told Jude.

'Go on then,' Jude replied.

'"Go on", what? What do you mean?' Cecilia questioned.

'Go on and on about *your* ex. It'd make me feel better for talking about Constance,' Jude clarified. Then he sighed. 'Actually, don't do that. I kind of demanded just then, and I didn't mean to do that. You don't have to talk about them,' Jude said.

It had been a long time since Cecilia had talked about Nicolas, the man who came to mind when she thought "ex". She wasn't sure if she wanted to talk about him. She wasn't even sure if she could. If she wanted to, and if she could, she felt like she couldn't ask for anyone better to talk to than Jude. She also felt like Trinity Café, with its eavesdropping patrons, wasn't the place to talk about Nicolas.

In front of Cecilia sat a full mug of cold cappuccino. She downed it in a few gulps. Once she'd emptied the mug, she returned it to the saucer, and Jude started chuckling.

'What are you laughing at?' Cecilia questioned.

'You have a little coffee foam moustache,' Jude told Cecilia.

Cecilia blushed. 'Oh no! I must look hideous!' she cried.

Jude shook his head. 'Nah. I don't think it's possible for you to look hideous,' he replied.

When Cecilia had bought the drinks, she'd been given napkins with them. Jude took one off his saucer and brushed Cecilia's upper lip with it. Where Jude had touched her through soft paper, Cecilia's skin tingled.

'Thank you,' Cecilia whispered.

'No problem,' Jude replied with a shrug.

For a moment, Cecilia gazed into Jude's grey eyes. Then she cleared her throat and asked: 'Can we go for a walk?'

'Yeah. That'd be great,' Jude agreed.

When Cecilia stood to go on the walk she'd proposed, she realised that it might be more challenging than she'd first thought thanks to her suddenly-weak knees.

*

CHAPTER TWENTY-NINE

The dozens of vehicles navigating the traffic lights at the west end of Colchester's High Street produced lots of fumes and made a great deal of noise. This bothered some of the pedestrians who also navigated the junction. Not Cecilia Bradley though, when she made her way past the junction with Jude, heading towards North Hill. This was because she was distracted from the unpleasant din and smell by Jude, who she was talking to about Nicolas, her ex-boyfriend.

'When Mum died, I became very introverted. I stopped paying attention to the world, including Nicolas. The only reason I managed to keep up with my course is that I knew Mum would've hated me to fail because of her. She was the first person I told when I realised proofreading was what I wanted to do for a career, and the first person I told when I signed up for a course to teach me how to do it. Every step of the way, she supported me,' Cecilia told Jude as they crossed from one side of Head Street to the other.

'Yeah, but you'd just lost your mum. You was bound to get quieter and more inside yourself while you dealt with it all in your head. That ain't an excuse for him to just go off to the other side of the country without a thought for you,' Jude said.

'It wasn't "without a thought for me". I think he moved to escape me. I was a nightmare back then. I didn't want to do anything or engage with anyone. All I did apart from my course was sit in my room and cry. When he came round to visit me, I didn't give him any affection. I simply cried on his shoulder. It definitely was *my* fault he ran away from me,' Cecilia replied.

By now, Jude and Cecilia were safely on the pavement heading down North Hill. Jude blocked the aforementioned pavement to stop Cecilia walking so he could look into her blue eyes. 'Nah, I don't agree with that. He gave you what, two months? It's your mum, who was your world. You ain't just gonna be all bright and happy two months after you've lost her. Well, maybe some people would be, but you can't just expect someone to just "get over it", or whatever. It ain't your fault he don't get grief,' Jude insisted.

Looking into Jude's eyes, Cecilia felt like the past itself had changed. It hadn't, of course, for Jude is not *The Terminator*, but her *perception* of the past had changed.

'Do you honestly think it wasn't my fault that Nicolas left me? Surely it's my fault? If I'd have shown him some love, he'd have stayed. Who'd want to stay with a woman who just cries and cries all the time?' Cecilia questioned.

'Yeah, but you wouldn't have been a woman who cries and cries *forever*. If he'd have just given you some time, perhaps you two could have stayed together. I mean, look at you now! A woman who's there for everyone, even people she's never met, who has a job that as far as I know, she's good at, who's always looking stunning, and who plays a mean game of snooker. I'm guessing you still have the odd cry every now and again, but don't we all? We might not admit it, but we do. That Nicolas bloke is missing out majorly,' Jude replied.

A man in a suit tutted and, with heavy footsteps, walked into the road to get around Jude and Cecilia. Neither of the people causing the obstruction that had bothered him so much noticed him.

'I'm sorry. I didn't mean to upset you again,' Jude said.

It was only then that Cecilia realised she was crying. At the same time, she realised that she was next to a busy road and lots of people could see her.

'These are happy tears but even so, I don't want the world seeing them. Can we go down this side street?' Cecilia asked, gesturing at a gap between an ordinary pub and an upmarket café.

When Jude nodded, he and Cecilia strode down the side road she'd gestured at, which seemed barely wide enough for a car.

-

At some point while walking down the side road, Cecilia's tears dried up. Conversation did too, but she felt comfortable with just the sound of hers and Jude's footsteps.

'What you said about me was most kind and sweet. Thank you,' Cecilia told Jude.

'It were true,' Jude replied with a shrug.

'You must think a lot of me to say such things. It feels nice to be around someone who likes me so much,' Cecilia said.

'Like I said, what I said about you is true. I don't *like* you though. That's not true. I *love* you,' Jude told Cecilia.

The word "love" seemed to disturb the rhythm of Cecilia's heart. 'You love me?' she questioned, trying to ignore the peculiar yet familiar feeling in her chest.

Jude chuckled. 'Yup. I am totally, dragonflies in stomach and all, in love with you. I have told you once before, in your car, but you didn't seem to hear the words,' he replied.

Before Cecilia could respond to the confirmation that Jude loved her, he sighed and said: 'I know you don't feel the same. That's cool, I get it. It don't stop me loving you though.'

'But I *do* love you! I have daydreamed about our future. About you messing my house up and me not caring because when I'm around you, I *don't* care. Well, I don't care about things like that. I care deeply about you, and myself, but not little things like what fabric conditioner is used for my towels,' Cecilia declared.

'Hang on a minute. *You* love *me*? Are you sure?' Jude questioned.

'Yes! You're kind, and fun, and effortless company. You see me like no-one else does. Of course I love you. You are most wonderful,' Cecilia enthused.

A smile spread across Jude's face. 'I could say the same about you, but not as nicely,' he replied.

While declaring their love for each other, Jude and Cecilia had ambled along the narrow side road, which ended with some ancient archways.

'What's all this?' Jude asked, gesturing at the reddish-brown archways of compacted clay and bricks.

'This is the Balkerne Gate. It's what remains of a Roman gateway from the first century,' Cecilia told Jude.

Cecilia walked under one of the archways and touched the wall. 'Thousands, maybe even millions of people have walked or rode under here. I can almost feel it,' she said.

When Jude joined Cecilia under the archway, he found he felt the same. 'In Cambridge, the history felt stuffy and unfriendly. I felt like the people from the past was frowning on me. Here, I feel like they're smiling,' he commented.

'I'm definitely smiling. It's nice to share this with you,' Cecilia replied with a grin.

It had been cloudy for most of Jude and Cecilia's walk from Trinity Café to the Balkerne Gate, but a sudden break in that cloud allowed bright sunlight to shine on Cecilia's glossy golden hair. That, combined with her smile, made Jude think she was even more beautiful than she usually was. Her beauty inspired him to do something.

'A young woman shared something magical with me once. Mind

if I share with you what she shared with me?' Jude asked.

'Erm, I guess not. I don't know what you're talking about, but I suppose I'll find out,' Cecilia replied.

When Jude took a step closer to her, Cecilia caught a whiff of his woody aftershave and was reminded of their first kiss. Jude then eased the lips Cecilia was now daydreaming about so close to hers that they were almost touching.

For a few seconds, Jude stood motionless, gazing into Cecilia's eyes. She could feel and smell his breath which, like hers, was warm, irregular, and smelt of coffee.

Because she was so focused on his mouth, Cecilia didn't realise Jude had his hands buried in her hair until he started gliding them through her curls. She felt those same hands gently encourage her to angle her head slightly to the right, and she obeyed. Cecilia now knew what Jude wanted to share with her, and her heart pumped hard, as if trying to escape her chest, in anticipation of what was to come.

When Jude finally kissed her, Cecilia let out a moan as soft as his lips. She closed her eyes and was aware of nothing but Jude, and what he was making her feel. One of the first things she felt was her knees weaken, but that was of no concern to her, as she had no intention of moving any time soon. The weather was mild, and Cecilia's flower print dress was quite thin, but she felt perfectly warm. The warmth had originated from her lips, and had spread throughout her body, relaxing her as it travelled.

In one sudden and disorientating jolt, Cecilia found herself cold and fully aware of her surroundings again. Upon opening her eyes, she established the cause of this was the four inch gap between her lips and Jude's.

'More,' Cecilia whispered.

The four inch gap was closed, and Cecilia was transported back to a world that was just her and Jude. She thought it was a familiar and predictable world, for the way Jude was kissing her mirrored how she had once kissed him. Much to her surprise and delight, she found it wasn't, for Jude introduced a new element that hadn't been present in their previous kisses.

Just as Cecilia was feeling so light-headed that she was seriously concerned about her ability to remain upright, Jude once again returned her to the real world.

'The coffee you had *does* taste good!' Cecilia cried, for it was the first thing that came into her head and all filters had been temporarily disabled.

Jude chuckled. 'Yeah, it does,' he agreed. Then he scratched his head and asked: 'Was it okay that I proper snogged you instead of just a light kiss?'

'Oh my goodness, yes! I did ask for more, after all, and you definitely gave me that!' Cecilia replied.

'I did. I wanted to. It just sort of felt right, you know?' Jude said.

It felt more than right to Cecilia, and her beaming smile showed that. 'That deserves repeating somewhere a bit more romantic than a Roman gateway at the end of a road,' she declared.

'Do you mean trying that place again?' Jude asked, pointing at The Tower's Shadow, a restaurant he knew Cecilia considered to be romantic.

Cecilia shook her head and said: 'I did not. I meant a venue that serves poor quality food, but is the perfect balance between casual and romantic.'

The promise of a date at a mystery location excited Jude almost as much as the kiss he'd just had. The literal forecast was cloudy, but the metaphorical forecast was sunnier than he had ever dreamed possible.

*

CHAPTER THIRTY

'Hello. I'd like, if you don't mind, to buy a dress to wear while I cook dinner for a man for the first time. I haven't done this before, so I don't know what one wears for this. I know that's not a helpful request for you, and I'm sorry, but I need help,' Cecilia told the woman with pursed lips who was standing behind the counter at Toothill's.

'Well, I'll need a bit more information to choose a dress for you. As you can see, we have a great deal of stock. I'm sure it can all be worn while cooking dinner for your boyfriend,' pursed lips woman replied.

In search of inspiration, Cecilia glanced over her shoulder at the sleeves of the dozens of dresses hanging on the rails. She saw nothing that was quite her.

When Cecilia had walked into Toothill's, she'd felt sure that she'd find an outfit that helped her stand tall and hold her head high. That confidence had evaporated as soon as pursed lips woman had opened her mouth.

'Yes, I guess so. Sorry for bothering you. I'll go,' Cecilia muttered at the dinked and scratched plywood floor.

'Well, that's your choice,' pursed lips woman said.

Without the dress she'd wanted so much, Cecilia turned and headed to the door, which creaked when she opened it. She didn't step through it because behind her, she heard the sound of heels tip-tapping at great pace across the hard floor.

'Lady with the amazing blonde hair! Hello again!' cried a familiar voice from behind Cecilia.

Cecilia closed the door and span round to see Eugenie rushing out from the stockroom behind the counter. 'Eugenie! Good to see you,' Cecilia said.

'Ah, thank you! You too,' Eugenie replied.

As if to show how happy she was to see Cecilia, Eugenie did a little twirl, sending her long and straight pastel pink hair flying into pursed lips woman's face.

'Well, what's got into you?' pursed lips woman asked Eugenie.

'Sorry, Auntie. I'm just so excited that I get to dress this lady again,' Eugenie said. Then she frowned and asked: 'Can I pick something for you, please? Is that why you are here?'

'I'd love you to. I'm going to invite a man over for dinner, and my cooking leaves a lot to be desired, so I need a dress to impress him. You did such a good job with my snooker outfit, so I'd appreciate your help,' Cecilia said.

Now Eugenie was on the case, Cecilia regained hope that she might leave the shop with a confidence-boosting outfit.

'Well, I guess I'm not needed then. I'll be out the back,' pursed lips woman told Eugenie. She slunk off into the stockroom without another word.

Now that her colleague was out of the way, Eugenie twirled again. She had a huge smile on her face.

'We had some dresses in yesterday, and one of them instantly made me think of you. Please may I show it to you?' Eugenie practically begged Cecilia.

'Of course,' Cecilia replied.

With a happy squeal and the tip-tapping of her high heels, Eugenie glided across the shop floor and plucked an emerald green velvet strappy evening gown from a rail. She stroked the fabric before holding it up for Cecilia to see.

'This is smart, conservative, classy, and impressive, as are you. It should suit you perfectly,' Eugenie said.

'It's so timeless!' Cecilia cried.

'Yes. We're very contemporary, so this isn't our usual stock. You're not our usual customer, which is why I thought of you when I saw the dress,' Eugenie explained.

'Thank you for thinking of me. I'll try it on,' Cecilia replied.

Before Cecilia could change her mind, Eugenie thrust the dress into her hand.

-

Two hours after she'd purchased it, Cecilia was admiring her new velvet dress. It looked even better in her bedroom mirror than it had in the mirror at Toothill's.

In the shop it came from, the dress had looked so good that Eugenie had burst into happy tears.

In Cecilia's bedroom, the dress looked so good that she plucked up the courage to dial Jude's landline from her house phone. The answer machine picked up, so she told it: 'I've made a reservation for us at eight o'clock on Friday at my dinner table. I look forward to seeing you there.'

*

CHAPTER THIRTY-ONE

When Cecilia let him into her home, the first thing Jude noticed was her dress and her hair.

'Wow! In the words of Morton: "you know how to dress". You know how to do your hair up too,' Jude commented.

'Like before, this wasn't me. Eugenie from one of the little boutiques in the Lanes chose this. I decided to put my hair up, but I only know how thanks to Emma-Leigh,' Cecilia replied with a smile.

'You're the one wearing it, and wearing it very well,' Jude pointed out.

The compliment made Cecilia colour a little bit.

'Why don't you follow me in? I've laid the table but you're early, so dinner isn't on yet,' Cecilia said.

As he was lead through Cecilia's house to her kitchen-diner, which was at the back, Jude admired the immaculate state of everything. There were shelves of books, all perfectly organised alphabetically by author's surname, and not a speck of dust anywhere to be seen. The air had a faint whiff of lavender thanks to discreet air fresheners in every room. Even the cushions on the sofa in the lounge, which Jude had to pass to get to the kitchen-diner, were perfectly plumped.

'You have a beautiful house,' Jude told Cecilia.

'I bought it with my inheritance from Mum, and Emma-Leigh helped me choose all the soft furnishings and how to lay out the furniture,' Cecilia replied.

Jude nodded, but did not say anything.

The moment she got into her kitchen, Cecilia started searching for ingredients in her cupboards. She found an as-yet-unopened jar of smoked paprika, which she placed on the black laminate worktop next to a brown paper bag of mushrooms, onions, and garlic that she'd bought from a greengrocers earlier in the day. From another cupboard, she took out soured cream and soy sauce.

'I need to cook now, and I can't chat while cooking because I get distracted and burn things. Sorry about that. Do you want me to put some music on to keep you entertained?' Cecilia said.

'I can't cook under any conditions, so don't worry about it. Some music would be cool though,' Jude replied.

'I was thinking of McFly, so I don't know how cool the music will be,' Cecilia told Jude.

'Never listened to them. I'd like to though,' Jude replied.

-

McFly kept Jude entertained while Cecilia cooked, creating mouth-watering smells.

When her food was ready, Cecilia slopped it into two bowls, which she put on the table that Jude was sitting at.

'Oh, I forgot to serve anything with it! I'm sorry!' Cecilia cried, only then remembering that she had intended to cook some rice to put on the side.

'It's cool. I mean, it's alright,' Jude replied with a shrug.

Cecilia picked up her shiny, streak-free cutlery and put it back down again without touching her food. She then picked up her glass and put it back down without drinking any wine.

Jude picked up his shiny, streak-free cutlery and used it to shovel stroganoff into his mouth.

'Mmm! This is good!' Jude cried once he had an empty mouth.

'It's Mum's recipe. She had a veggie phase and during it, this was her favourite dish,' Cecilia told Jude.

After eating another mouthful, Jude asked: 'So you just cooked me what at one time was your mum's favourite food?'

'Yes. She loved this. It's the only dish that everyone in my family can make. She used to say that I made it the best, but I think she was just being nice,' Cecilia replied.

Before answering, Jude wolfed down yet more of the stroganoff. 'I ain't ate it cooked by anyone else, but I'm pretty sure your mum weren't just being nice. This is, hands down, the best veggie thing I've ever eaten. It's one of the best things I've ever eaten, full stop. It's special too, to know this was your mum's favourite. I get how much it means to share this, and I'm totally grateful,' he said.

'I think she'd be pleased that I shared it with you. I like to think she'd have approved of us, had she have got the chance to meet you,' Cecilia replied.

'Do you think so? I'm nothing special. I'm just a painter and decorator who don't even speak proper English,' Jude questioned.

'All Mum wanted for me, *and* Conner, was someone who made us happy. Wealth, employment, background, manner of speaking, even gender, none of it mattered to her. You make me happy, so she'd have liked you. It's that simple,' Cecilia insisted.

Jude smiled. 'I think I'd have liked your mum. If I'd have got to meet her, I'd have thanked her for raising such a great daughter, and I'd have told her she makes me happy,'

Only when Cecilia didn't answer did Jude realise she was crying. He jumped up and awkwardly cuddled her. This just made her cry more.

'I'm sorry, Cecilia. I didn't mean to upset you,' Jude whispered in her ear.

'Don't be sorry. I loved talking about her. I never get to. Conner and I aren't close enough for us to share our memories, and I don't think Dad can bare to talk about her. I *want* to talk about her though. It helps. It keeps part of her alive,' Cecilia replied.

When Cecilia sniffed loudly and swept her napkin off the table, Jude released her and returned to his seat. Cecilia used her napkin to blow her nose, and then she shook her head. 'It is me who should be sorry. I love talking about Mum, but getting all teary isn't ideal on a date. You're nice to listen,' she said.

'A date is about learning more about the other person. Your mum is a part of you. I wanna know about her. I wanna eat food she taught you how to make too,' Jude replied.

Talking about her mum had made Cecilia forget all about the food she'd cooked. She glanced down at her untouched mushroom stroganoff, which was still warm. 'Let's eat up then,' she suggested.

-

The food was so good that it completely absorbed Jude and Cecilia's attention. They forgot about each other and their glasses of wine. They were so absorbed that when Cecilia's phone started buzzing, they both jumped.

'I'm sorry about this. Let me just dismiss this call,' Cecilia said. She strode over to the sideboard, where her phone was sitting, to reject the call, but frowned when she saw the name on screen. 'Tamsyn? Why is she calling?' Cecilia questioned aloud.

'Find out if you like. She's your best mate. I get it,' Jude replied.

The moment Jude told her she could, Cecilia jabbed the green circle on her phone screen.

'Tamsyn! Is everything alright?' Cecilia asked, hiding all traces of annoyance.

When she heard Tamsyn's reply, Cecilia gasped. 'Oh, you poor thing. That must have been horrible! I can't imagine walking in on that!' she cried.

When some people can only hear one end of a conversation, their imagination tries to fill in the other side. That was the case with Jude. He was trying to work out what Tamsyn had walked in on.

While Jude's imagination was working overtime, Cecilia was listening to Tamsyn. 'Don't be silly! Ian was right to tell you to call me,' she told her in answer to what she'd said.

Jude could tell that Tamsyn was arguing, because Cecilia was shaking her head. 'It's okay, Tamsyn. Your place isn't suitable to discuss this in, so I'll be waiting for you when you get home to take you to mine. I have a spare room, so you can stay the night,' Cecilia said.

By now, Jude was wondering if Tamsyn had walked in on a debt collection letter. Cecilia struck him as the kind of person who, even though she didn't have much spare cash, would help friends in need.

'No arguments, Tamsyn. You've been through hell, so I'm going to help you process it. It's the least I can do,' Cecilia insisted.

The firm tone Cecilia used with her friend made Jude chuckle. She was the kind of person who helped her friends, whether they liked it or not.

Using a much warmer tone, Cecilia said goodbye to Tamsyn and put her mobile back on the side.

'I need to go and pick up Tamsyn. I'll drop you home on the way to Chelmsford,' Cecilia told Jude.

'But...' Jude started to protest.

'Sorry Jude, she needs me. I have to take you home and then go and get her,' Cecilia replied, cutting him off.

'But...' Jude protested again.

'Look, I wanted this date as much as you, but my best friend desperately needs me! No argument you can make will make me abandon her in her hour of need! Now shut up and let me take you home!' Cecilia snapped, once again not allowing Jude to finish his sentence.

Because he'd been told to shut up, Jude didn't answer Cecilia, and he didn't say a word for the whole of his tense journey home in Cecilia's Mini.

*

CHAPTER THIRTY-TWO

When Cecilia plonked herself down on the sofa and gestured at the armchair she usually sat in, Tamsyn was confused. She sat down next to Cecilia on the sofa.

'You've had an awful day. Have the armchair,' Cecilia told Tamsyn.

Any thought of protesting left Tamsyn's head when she sank into Cecilia's armchair. 'So comfy! It's like being hugged by furniture,' she murmured.

'Now you're sitting comfortably, shall we begin?' Cecilia suggested.

'Are you sure about this? It's dark and disturbing,' Tamsyn questioned.

'Definitely. I'm sure your mentor has explained the benefits of talking about trauma. I imagine he's at home talking to his wife about it now,' Cecilia confirmed.

Because Cecilia was so insistent, and she knew she had to, Tamsyn drew a deep breath to tell her friend what she'd seen.

'We got a call to a twenty-one-year-old male. Ian was driving. The patient's boss, concerned for his welfare after not being able to contact him, had visited his home address. He got no response when he hammered on the door, so he forced entry into the property and found the patient in his bedroom, displaying no signs of life,' Tamsyn told Cecilia.

Already, Cecilia could guess how the story ended. 'Oh, Tamsyn,' she whispered.

'It was simply not possible to resuscitate the patient. We believe he passed away yesterday evening. Cause of death, or rather, suspected cause of death, was easy to establish because the patient had left us a note,' Tamsyn said.

'Overdose?' Cecilia asked.

On the coffee table next to the armchair Tamsyn was sitting in was a pen, which she picked up and rolled between her fingers. She gazed at the pen in detail for a few seconds, studying the squircle lid.

'Tamsyn?' Cecilia said when her friend didn't answer.

'I couldn't help but read the note when I saw it. It started with an apology to whoever found him, and the ambulance service, who he knew would be called. I don't remember the note verbatim, though I read it several times, but I remember the sentence: "I am disgusting, depraved, and perverted (so I'm told), I don't deserve to live (so I'm told), so now I'm not living (so you've discovered)". When I read that bit, I thought the man must be some kind of sex offender. I thought he must have ended his life because he felt guilty about whatever he'd done. That wasn't the case at all. I read on, and it turns out his family said those things to him because he's gay. He killed himself because he didn't know how to live in a world where his family said such vile things about him and no-one understood him,' Tamsyn replied.

'Oh, Tamsyn! That poor man! Poor you for having to attend that!' Cecilia cried.

The pen Tamsyn had picked up was still in her hands, and she was twirling it as if she was doing a baton display but had forgotten her baton, so was using a pen instead.

'That could have been me,' Tamsyn murmured, transferring the pen to her left hand.

'What do you mean?' Cecilia questioned.

'If it wasn't for you, it could have been me who took God knows how many boxes of paracetamol, just because I didn't know how to live in this world,' Tamsyn explained.

In a few seconds, all of Cecilia's previous interactions with Tamsyn flashed through her mind. In none of them did she see any signs that Tamsyn didn't know how to live in the world she found herself in.

'I had no idea you felt that way,' Cecilia whispered.

'I don't *now*. I haven't had such thoughts for over a year, which is such a relief. They pestered me throughout my teens,' Tamsyn replied.

Cecilia recalled how happy Tamsyn had seemed when she'd bought her cream tea on the day they met. The pair of them had talked for hours, and Tamsyn had shared with her that she was asexual. Cecilia remembered thinking at the time that it was unusual for someone to be so open with a stranger. Now she realised it might have been because Tamsyn had nothing to lose.

'Were you planning to take your life on the day we met?' Cecilia asked.

'I got a text from my mother a few days before we met. It asked what the point of life was without love. I thought she made a good point. I was thinking of doing something over the holidays, so that the university didn't immediately notice something was amiss. When you started talking to me, you were so nice, as was the cream tea you bought me, that I began to wonder why I was considering leaving this world behind. I told you I was asexual because I thought you'd be abusive and remind me why I was thinking about something so drastic. Of course, you weren't abusive. You were understanding. I reconsidered, and now I'm sat here today,' Tamsyn replied.

'I can't believe I didn't see it. I had no idea. Do you promise me you don't have these thoughts anymore?' Cecilia said.

'You didn't see it because you weren't supposed to. I hid it, like everything else about me. I can promise that I haven't had suicidal thoughts for over a year now, but that doesn't mean they're gone forever. After meeting you, I was happier than I'd ever been, but I still had suicidal thoughts. They hung around for ages. I just ignored them. Should they return, which they may well do, I'm much better placed to handle them now. Staff at my university and the ambulance service know I've had issues in the past, so hopefully they'd notice if something was up with me. Now you know, so you'd notice too. I'm not going to do anything, Cecilia. I know life is worth living, and there is help out there if you feel otherwise. That's why this young man's death upset me so much. If only he'd have reached out to the right places, this tragedy could have been prevented,' Tamsyn told Cecilia.

At some point while listening to Tamsyn, Cecilia felt something wet and warm on her cheek. She brushed her cheek with her hand and realised she was crying.

'Sorry. I came over here, interrupting whatever you were doing, and made you cry,' Tamsyn said.

With a large tissue from her coffee table, Cecilia dried her eyes. She then blew her nose with it.

'You don't need to apologise. I knew whatever you had to talk about would be upsetting, but it's important to talk about it. I wish I could make it so you never think these things again, but I can't. I'm here for you though, if you need me,' Cecilia replied.

'That's all I need. All I need is someone to be there. Someone to talk to,' Tamsyn said.

There was nothing more Tamsyn had to say about the incident she'd witnessed or the memories it had dragged up. She was satisfied that she'd shared all that she wanted to share.

With her mind freed from the weight of the feelings the incident she'd seen had promoted, Tamsyn was free to wonder what Cecilia had been up to before she'd called her. 'What did I interrupt?'

she asked.

Cecilia sighed and replied: 'Dinner with Jude, but don't worry about it. He showed his true colours when you called, and I wasn't impressed. You've saved me months of falling deeper and deeper in love with him only to find he's a selfish and self-centred arse.'

*

CHAPTER THIRTY-THREE

Colchester has a variety of independent eateries for people to meet in. It also has a variety of chain eateries. Cecilia chose one of the latter to meet Conner in.

'Was there a two-for-one offer on?' Conner questioned when he sat down with Cecilia, as she'd asked him to do.

'No. I simply thought this would be a good place to discuss Dad's party, among other things,' Cecilia replied.

In answer to this, Conner sipped some of his strawberry milk-shake.

Undeterred by Conner's silence, Cecilia decided to answer the question he wouldn't ask. 'I'm not going to help with Dad's party. He doesn't need a big bash and even if he did, I couldn't organise it with you. Your behaviour isn't conducive to a productive working relationship,' she told him.

'He'll be so disappointed when we don't do anything special for his birthday. I can't force you to help though. Mum would've done it, but I can't bring her back to do it,' Conner replied.

'I doubt he'll be that disappointed. Whatever we'd have done, it wouldn't have made him forget his wife isn't there,' Cecilia pointed out.

From a bright red carton, Conner plucked a fry, which he popped in his mouth and chewed leisurely, slowly releasing its salty and oily flavour.

'Is there anything you'd like to say to me?' Cecilia asked.

Conner shook his head and put another fry in his mouth.

'Now that I've talked to you about Dad's party, I'd like to discuss our relationship going forward,' Cecilia said.

'What are you suggesting, incest?' Conner questioned.

'No!' Cecilia snapped. She took a deep breath and explained: 'I meant that I want to see you less often.'

'Oh, so you want to estrange me. I see,' Conner replied.

Although she'd anticipated it, Conner's behaviour still bothered Cecilia. It didn't bother her enough to make her mess up though. She had a plan for the meeting, and she was determined to stick to it.

'I don't want us to be *estranged*, simply more distant. It doesn't do me any good seeing you. You don't treat me how I deserve to be treated. You're only young, so I have hope that you'll grow out of it. Until you do, we should see less of each other,' Cecilia told Conner.

'Dad will be upset, and I can't imagine what Mum would've said,' Conner said.

'Dad will only know if you tell him, and Mum wouldn't have said anything,' Cecilia replied.

As he couldn't think of anything to say to that, Conner rummaged through the brown paper bag in front of him in search of his quarter-pound burger. When he found it, he placed it on the table, next to his paper bag, and stared at the cardboard box it was in.

'Do you really get that upset about the things I say to you?' Conner asked.

'The way you behave towards me is most upsetting,' Cecilia replied.

'I don't mean it to be. If I meant to upset you, I'd try harder. It's just meant to be funny,' Conner told Cecilia.

'That's what you always say when I challenge you, but it's possible to be funny without being hurtful. I know a man who has made me laugh many times, a few times because he has teased me. I've never been upset by any of the jokes he's made. Confused, sometimes, but not hurt,' Cecilia replied.

Cecilia had ordered a box of chicken nuggets. She nibbled one and her mouth watered when she tasted the juicy chicken and crispy batter.

'I didn't mean to upset you, little sister! Don't get all huffy about it, please,' Conner begged.

'I'm not. My response to the way you treat me is proportional and rational,' Cecilia replied.

'Then don't cut me out of your life,' Conner said.

'I'm not. I'm reducing your part in it. Should your behaviour improve, it will be my pleasure to increase your role in my world. After all, you are Mum's son. It is in my interests to have a relationship with you, but it must be a healthy one,' Cecilia pointed out.

Having silenced Conner once again, Cecilia treated herself to a whole nugget. It was so good that she closed her eyes so she could focus all her attention on the pleasing texture and flavour in her mouth.

Even after Cecilia had finished savouring her nugget, Conner hadn't spoken. He hadn't done anything. He'd just sat still, in silence.

'Isn't your food getting cold?' Cecilia questioned.

'Erm, yes. It is actually. I should eat it,' Conner replied.

-

Food rendered Conner and Cecilia speechless, and they pretty much remained that way until they parted ways. That, and the food itself, left Cecilia with a feeling of immense satisfaction.

*

CHAPTER THIRTY-FOUR

The key safe at Mr Wight's house was difficult to find, unless, like Emma-Leigh, you'd been told where to look for it. Even though she'd used it countless times, Emma-Leigh still had to rummage around in the wisteria for a few seconds to locate the key safe. When she did, she always cheered in her head before inputting the code and removing the old-fashioned barrel key.

Just before Emma-Leigh could insert the key in the front door, Mr Wight opened it, making her jump.

'Oh, sorry for the fright, young Miss Layton! I forgot to tell you that I'm home today!' Mr Wight cried, jolly as ever, when he saw his cleaner standing before him.

'Calling me young more than makes up for it, Mr Wight,' Emma-Leigh replied with a smile.

'I've got a young lad painting me front room today, so I've left the office in the hopefully capable hands of my son. Don't worry if you cannot clean the front room properly today because of the decorator. Just do what you can and that,' Mr Wight volunteered.

Emma-Leigh nodded. 'Thank you, Mr Wight,' she said.

Having greeted Emma-Leigh, Mr Wight showed her into the home she usually had to herself.

'This here is Austen, who's turning my magnolia walls white for me. Austen, this is Emma-Leigh Layton. *Young Miss* Emma-Leigh

Layton,' Mr Wight said as he entered the front room. The decorator who Mr Wight thought was called Austen pulled an expression that he couldn't read. 'It is Austen, isn't it?' he questioned.

'Yup, that's me. The name's Austen; Jude Austen,' Jude replied.

'Ah, good. I thought I was going senile for a moment there,' Mr Wight said.

'You, senile? Never, Mr Wight,' Emma-Leigh told him.

Mr Wight smiled. 'You are a sweetheart, Miss Layton,' he replied.

Being called a sweetheart made Emma-Leigh smile even wider than Mr Wight.

With introductions complete, Mr Wight said: 'I'll be making tea now. I like to do it before you make the kitchen all shiny.'

When Mr Wight had left the room, Jude asked: 'What are the chances? Us two working in the same house?'

'Not low enough, evidently,' Emma-Leigh replied with her hands on her hips.

This response confused Jude. 'What have I done? Cecilia won't answer my calls and you're in a mood with me?' he questioned.

'Do you honestly need me to tell you?' Emma-Leigh asked.

'I do! I can't for the life of me work out what I've done. I thought something might be up with Tamsyn, and that's why she weren't answering me, but what with the attitude you're giving me, I figure that I've done something,' Jude replied.

Emma-Leigh sighed. 'How about arguing when her best friend needed her? I dare say you were disappointed that your night was cut short, but Tamsyn was in Cecilia's life long before you. It is out of order to expect Cecilia to abandon her in her hour of need in favour of you, a virtual stranger,' she said.

'What? I *were* disappointed that the night weren't gonna end how I'd hoped, but I didn't expect Cecilia to abandon Tamsyn. In fact, I loved that she didn't put me before her friends. I thought that that dinner meant as much to her as it did to me, so I were impressed that she'd give it up for a friend in need. All it told me were that the dragonflies in my stomach was warranted,' Jude told Emma-Leigh.

'Dragonflies? Do you mean butterflies?' Emma-Leigh questioned.

'Oh, yeah! That were what I meant,' Jude confirmed.

While Emma-Leigh was chortling about Jude's mistake, Mr Wight entered the room with two mugs of tea, which he placed on the mahogany coffee table.

'I'm glad to see you're getting on well. I'll leave you to it,' Mr Wight said to the people he was paying to do jobs for him.

Without one word about wasting time, Mr Wight left the room again.

'I *know* you argued when Cecilia said she was taking you home to get Tamsyn. She told me so,' Emma-Leigh told Jude.

'Yeah, I did. There were no need for her to take me home,' Jude replied.

'Of course there was! Tamsyn wouldn't have felt comfortable talking with you there,' Emma-Leigh pointed out.

'That weren't what I meant. I meant that Cecilia didn't have to take me home. I could've got a cab or something. It would've saved her time,' Jude explained.

Suddenly, Emma-Leigh began to question the tale her friend had told her. Something didn't add up. Until she could work out what had happened, she didn't feel like she could say another word.

'She wouldn't let me tell her not to take me home. I tried to tell her, but all I got to say were: "but". She kept cutting me off,' Jude explained without being asked to.

That one revelation was the missing piece of the puzzle that Emma-Leigh needed to make everything make sense.

'Oh, Cecilia. You're as blind as your name suggests,' Emma-Leigh murmured.

'What?' Jude questioned.

'Cecilia means: "blind",' Emma-Leigh explained. The moment she said that, a contradictory memory popped into her head. 'Actually, it might mean: "blind to one's own beauty". I'm not sure,' Emma-Leigh said.

'She's *totally* the latter,' Jude commented.

'She's the former, too. She genuinely thinks you didn't want her to go to Tamsyn. Based on that, she's decided that you're a selfish arse,' Emma-Leigh replied.

Jude shook his head. Everything seemed to be such a muddle. A muddle he desperately wanted to solve, but didn't know how. Cecilia wouldn't answer his calls. He thought about just turning up on her doorstep, but it seemed so invasive, and like something out of one of the rom-com's that Floyd loved watching.

While Jude was thinking deeply, so was Emma-Leigh. She was forming plans.

'Why are you pouting?' Jude asked Emma-Leigh.

'I do that when I think,' Emma-Leigh explained.

'What you thinking about?' Jude asked.

'I'm thinking about how to get you and Cecilia back together,' Emma-Leigh revealed.

-

Because they were both being paid to work, Jude and Emma-Leigh stopped chatting to do just that.

While cleaning, Emma-Leigh pouted lots. Thanks to the mirrored sideboard she was meticulously cleaning, she could see herself doing it.

When Emma-Leigh thought she'd finished cleaning the sideboard, Jude called to her: 'You missed a spot.'

In response, Emma-Leigh strolled from the hallway she'd been working in into the adjoining front room, where she saw three white walls and one magnolia one. 'So did you,' Emma-Leigh told Jude, pointing at the magnolia wall.

'I'll deal with it. I'm in no hurry. I'm cool as a courgette,' Jude replied.

'As a what?' Emma-Leigh questioned.

'Oh, it ain't a courgette, is it?!' Jude cried.

Emma-Leigh chortled. 'Most people would say *cucumber*, but then you're not most people. That's what makes you perfect for Cecilia, and that's why I'm going to get you two back together,' she replied.

*

CHAPTER THIRTY-FIVE

Thanks to prior research, Emma-Leigh found Stockwell Street Food, where Cecilia had asked to meet up, with ease. The moment she stepped through the door, the lime green and canary yellow walls assaulted her eyes. This was unexpected, for in pictures on Stockwell Street Food's website, the walls had been white.

The tables, which were white, gave Emma-Leigh's eyes welcome respite. She scanned them and saw Cecilia waiting for her at the back of the room.

'The paint choices here are questionable, aren't they?' Emma-Leigh said in greeting to Cecilia.

'I like them. They're bright and cheerful,' Cecilia replied.

'Seems like it's not just the walls that are bright and cheerful,' Emma-Leigh commented.

As if to confirm that she was indeed bright and cheerful, Cecilia grinned. 'I'm having a good week. I've dealt with Conner, I've got a new monthly contract with a local magazine, and now I'm having lunch with you,' she said.

It surprised Emma-Leigh that her friend was so happy. 'What happened between you and Jude wasn't good,' she pointed out.

For a second or two, Cecilia's blue eyes lost their sparkle, and the corners of her mouth turned down. When she regained her upbeat demeanour, her smile was wider, and her tone was more animated. 'No, it wasn't! His behaviour was completely out of order!' she cried.

'You must have been so disappointed,' Emma-Leigh murmured.

Once again, Cecilia's smile temporarily disappeared. She put it back on as swiftly as she could, but Emma-Leigh noticed and read the expression that appeared in its absence. 'It's definitely his loss though,' she replied.

Not sure what to say next, Emma-Leigh gazed out of the window she was sitting by. There wasn't much to see; just a man in a grey paint-splattered hoodie who she knew was looking into the restaurant while trying to hide the fact that he was looking into the restaurant.

'Jude was always punching above his weight, trying to get you, but I thought you liked him. Won't you miss him?' Emma-Leigh questioned.

'No,' Cecilia answered without a moment's hesitation.

That single word seemed to make Emma-Leigh's tummy bubble and her breathing get faster.

'Didn't you like him? You enthused about what good company he was, and whenever I asked if you wanted to kiss him, you got all girly and shy. Did you not once go on and on about how kind he was because he flew over to Cambridge to help his sister with something?' Emma-Leigh asked.

'But he's *not* kind! I thought he was, but he wasn't! I was wrong, and he's an arse, so stop taunting me!' Cecilia snapped.

The volume of Cecilia's voice attracted attention from her fellow diners.

'Sorry. I didn't mean to shout,' Cecilia said to Emma-Leigh and everyone else in earshot.

Once their fellow diners were once again focused on their plates of pasta, Emma-Leigh asked Cecilia: 'What did Jude do? I remember it was to do with you having to cut your date short to help Tamsyn, but I've forgotten the details. Can you remind me?'

'When I told him I had to go, he argued. That's unacceptable. Tamsyn needed me and...' Cecilia started to say. She paused when Emma-Leigh raised a hand.

'You say he argued and it was unacceptable. What exactly did he say?' Emma-Leigh asked.

'He didn't get to say anything. Well, he got to say: "but". The moment I realised he was going to make a fuss, I decided to put a stop to it. It wasn't even *Lia* who stood up to him. It was plain old me,' Cecilia explained.

A quick glance out the window told Emma-Leigh the man wearing the paint-splattered hoodie was still there. He was shifting his weight from foot to foot and looking at his digital watch. She smiled at him and turned her attention back to Cecilia.

'So Jude *didn't* argue. He just tried to say *something* and you cut him off. For all you know, he was going to say: "But what about the roadworks on the A twelve?". That wouldn't be arguing, and it would be perfectly acceptable,' Emma-Leigh pointed out.

Cecilia's head fell into her hands. 'Oh, I'm an idiot! I never thought of that! Emma-Leigh, when he got out of the Mini to walk down the street, I glared at him! I've been ignoring his calls, I've bad-mouthed him to you and Tamsyn, and I've spent this whole week thinking of him as an arse!' she cried.

'Now you know he wasn't arguing, do you want Jude back?' Emma-Leigh asked.

'One hundred percent yes! If only it was possible, I'd apologise right here, right now, and beg him to forgive me,' Cecilia replied.

Emma-Leigh breathed a huge sigh of relief. 'Thank goodness for that,' she said.

'Why? He's not here. I had my plan of being friends for a bit to be sure I wanted him, and then just as I found that I *did* want him, I messed it up. Now we're not even friends! I've messed it all up,' Cecilia replied.

In response, Emma-Leigh gestured out of the window at the man in the paint-splattered hoodie. The man flipped his hood back to reveal a mop of brown curls. With his face now recognisable, the man strolled across the street, towards Stockwell Street Food.

When Cecilia spotted the man, she gasped. 'Oh, Emma-Leigh! Whatever you've done, thank you! Thank you times a million!' she cried.

By the time the man in the paint-splattered hoodie reached her table, Cecilia was crying, so all she could say was: 'Jude. I'm most sorry.'

Jude shrugged and took a seat between Cecilia and Emma-Leigh. 'It's cool. I'm just glad you know now, that's all,' he replied.

'I saw him on a cleaning job. He was painting magnolia walls white. I was frosty with him, he asked why, and it became clear there had been a misunderstanding. The moment I realised there'd been a mistake, I resolved to get you two back together. Thanks to our regular lunch dates, that was simple,' Emma-Leigh explained.

The mention of the job he'd been working on when he'd bumped into Emma-Leigh reminded Jude of something. 'That man, Mr Wight, called me a couple of days ago. I thought something were wrong, but it turned out he just wanted to thank me for doing a good job. I ain't had that before. It were weird, but nice,' he told Emma-Leigh.

'That's very him,' Emma-Leigh replied with a smile.

'Jude, I can't apologise enough. I can't imagine what you must think of me,' Cecilia said, ignoring the exchange between him and Emma-Leigh.

'Nah, I don't think you can imagine what I think of you,' Jude replied.

Even though she dreaded hearing the answer, Cecilia asked: 'What do you think of me?'

'I think you're the cleverest but kindest woman I've ever met. I think you worry too much, especially when it comes to yourself. I think you're a great friend. I think you're super organised. I think my life would be a trillion percent better with you in it,' Jude told Cecilia. Then, Jude grinned and said: 'I think other things about you too, but I ain't gonna discuss them in a restaurant in front of your friend.'

Yet more tears escaped Cecilia's eyes, but she didn't mind, for they were tears of joy.

'Does this mean we're a couple? Do you still want that?' Cecilia questioned.

'Yup. I've wanted it since our eyes met across a snooker table, and now I've got it; we're a couple,' Jude confirmed.

The knowledge that she and Jude were an item put a radiant smile on Cecilia's face. It also prompted a personality shift.

'Right, Emma-Leigh, thank you for all that you've done, but I'd like to make plans with Jude for tonight, so can you leave us to it, please?' Cecilia asked.

'Ooh, saucy!' Emma-Leigh replied, getting up to do what she'd been asked to do.

Once Emma-Leigh had left the building, Cecilia guffawed and commented to Jude: 'I don't know what she's thinking. I don't plan that sort of thing.'

Partly at Emma-Leigh's expense, Jude and Cecilia laughed together. They then went on to make plans for the night (which did not involve anything saucy), and catch up.

-

'It was simply that she'd witnessed a traumatic incident. She has to talk to someone about these events, and as she's estranged from her family and has no partner, I'm the person she talks to about what she sees,' Cecilia explained when Jude enquired about Tamsyn's welfare.

'Like I said, you're a good friend. That shows it,' Jude said.

'You're a good friend too, to ask after her when you barely know her,' Cecilia pointed out.

'Thanks,' Jude replied with a grin.

When Cecilia took a sip from her cup of coffee, she found it was full and stone cold. She downed it anyway, because talking lots had made her thirsty.

Once her cup was empty, Cecilia said: 'There's simply one more thing to sort out; who's music will we listen to while I cook?'

EPILOGUE

One year after...

An empty plate that had once contained sticky BBQ chicken wings sat in front of Cecilia. To the right of Cecilia's plate was a half-eaten fillet steak on a slate, across from it was an almost empty plate of buttermilk chicken, and to the side of *that* was a burger on a wooden chopping board.

'It's so nice to be off my feet, enjoying good food and better company,' Tamsyn commented when she'd polished off her plate of chicken.

'I feel the same. Rare that either of us get a chance to sit down, ain't it, Miss Tamsyn Menadue BA (Hons)? Not that I'm claiming being a painter and decorator is as hard as being a paramedic, even though I do seem to work for the most demanding firm in the world,' Jude replied after swallowing a mouthful of steak.

'It is very rare that I get a moment to even breathe, but I couldn't be happier with my life,' Tamsyn confirmed.

'Neither could I,' Jude said, looking to his left.

Looking down at her pink blouse, Cecilia decided she didn't feel the same as Jude and Tamsyn. '*I* could be happier, if Jude learnt not to mix colours in the washing machine,' she said

'If that is the worst thing Jude has done, then let me tell you, you are lucky,' Morton told Cecilia.

'It isn't, actually. I'd say that always leaving his trainers where I can trip over them is the worst thing he does,' Cecilia replied.

Jude blushed. 'Sorry,' he said.

Cecilia grinned and ruffled Jude's curly brown hair. 'It's okay. Whatever you do, I still love sharing my house with you,' she told him.

'Once I've got this down me, we'll pop upstairs and you can share a snooker table,' Morton said.

This reminded Tamsyn why the four of them had gathered in Thierry's Steakhouse and Grill at The Colneside. She raised her glass of lemonade and cried: 'Happy anniversary!'

It was indeed a happy anniversary. A happy anniversary for a happy couple.

ACKNOWLEDGEMENTS

I'd like to start by thanking Heidi Swain, Sarah Morgan, Leigh Bardugo, Ian McEwan, Andy Weir, and Lucy Worsley for writing acknowledgements at the end of their books, thus showing me how its done. Thanks to Steph, her son Theo, and her friend, my mum, for finding a way for me to put these acknowledgements and the preceding novel before your eyes. Thanks to all the people involved in the 2021 Masters snooker tournament, which I was watching when I came up with the idea for this book. Thanks to all the people who listened to me tell them made-up stories over the years. Thanks to all the people involved in making my dozens of notebooks and pens, which saved the ears of anyone I talked to for more than five minutes. Thanks to all the people involved in making Microsoft Word, which provided me with a way of writing a novel that I could upload to Kindle Direct Publishing (notebooks aren't accepted by KDP). Thanks to The Asexuality Visibility and Education Network, Stonewall, the BBC, Anglia Ruskin University, Colchester Borough Council, Cambridgeshire Live, and Google Maps, for having useful and informative websites that I used for research. Thanks to Mum, for giving me time to write this, giving up her own time to discuss various parts of this book, being the first person to read this book, and liking this book. Thank you to Mum for countless things that have nothing to do with this book. Finally, thank you to you, for reading this. I hope you enjoyed reading it as much as I enjoyed writing it.

Printed in Great Britain
by Amazon